# Nejla

# Nejla

## Bob & Barbara Hitching

**STL Books**
PO Box 48, Bromley, Kent, England
PO Box 28, Waynesboro, Georgia, USA
PO Box 656, Bombay 1, India

© 1984 Bob and Barbara Hitching
Second impression 1984

STL Books are published by Send The Light (Operation
Mobilisation), PO Box 48, Bromley, Kent, England.

ISBN 0 903843 79 X

Covers printed by Penderel Press Ltd, Croydon, Surrey.

Made and printed by
Hunt Barnard Printing Ltd, Aylesbury, Bucks.

*To Charissa, our little flower,
now in God's garden*

Our grateful appreciation goes to Krista Clark, who laboured as our secretary, faithfully coping with all the retypings of the manuscript. Also, our love and appreciation goes to Ken Anderson, who has believed in us and encouraged us to attempt new things.

# CONTENTS

# 1

# *The discovery*

The light filtered through the curtains into Nejla's bedroom. She stirred, then rolled over. The sudden jarring pain in her shoulder made her come awake abruptly. The dull, yet intense pain caused her to remember sadly the events of the previous day. The light that tumbled into her room was a reminder of yet another day to live, yet another day to survive somehow in the complexities of her home.

Gingerly she eased onto her back and stared at the ceiling. Her mind raced back to the long nights that she remembered as a child; the way a slight creak or noise outside would fill her heart with fear. Yet those long nights would almost be welcome now, as thoughts of her father, so quick to lash out at her, filled her mind.

She squeezed her eyes closed tightly as if trying to blot out the memories of the previous day. Hoping to escape the pain, she decided to concentrate on some of the joyful moments that she had experienced

recently. As her mind drifted, the good moments
seemed to act like a soothing ointment on her feelings
of rejection.

It had been two months ago that, to her surprise,
her father had agreed that she could visit her aunt in a
city some distance away. The morning she was to
leave passed in a bustle of activity. Trying to pack
all the presents she was to give to relatives into her
little suitcase seemed an impossible task. Then there
was a constant stream of visitors sending little par-
cels of food to their own relatives living in the same
city.

As Nejla pulled her suitcase up the one large step
onto the bus, a sense of relief and anticipation
flooded over her, and the tension that had built up in
her melted away. The bus was crowded, smoky and
noisy. She remembered looking at the driver, who
seemed so aloof and distant. Absent-mindedly, she
glanced across to the little cloth with tassles hanging
from the mirror by the driver's seat; *'Inshallah'* ('If
God wills it') was embroidered on the little circular
piece of green cloth.

'If God wills it'! For a moment she felt a strange
feeling inside her. She had seen the words more times
than she could remember, but suddenly their
significance hit her. Is there a God who actually has a
plan for individual people? The thought was both
provoking and stimulating.

The driver sounded his horn loudly and the bus
moved off round the corner. Nejla was jolted back
from her thoughts of God's will to the sudden
realisation that she was leaving her small town. It was
the first time that she had ever gone any great distance

from her home, and now at sixteen years old she was on her way to an adventure.

Arriving at her aunt's house was an adventure almost in itself. Her relatives were at the bus station to greet her. There were hugs, laughter, kisses, and a lot of excited chattering. Nejla could barely take in all the new sights and sounds she was experiencing; the crowded bus station, people shouting and rushing to and fro. Even the car ride back to her aunt's house was full of new things to see.

Once greetings had been completed, and tea drunk, her cousin Gulden showed Nejla her bedroom. She carefully unpacked her suitcase, putting the gifts she had brought for her relatives and friends into neat piles.

Her aunt, Hanife, lived in a block of flats on a busy street. Hanife's husband had left her some years before and she had struggled on to raise a family of five girls. Some of the local rumours suggested that her husband had left her because she had never given him a son.

Nejla loved her cousins even though they had only met once before, when they had all come to her small town for her grandfather's funeral.

Gulden was the oldest of her cousins, two years older than Nejla. As they all sat at the dinner table, Nejla noticed that something was different about Gulden, something she couldn't identify and yet that was very obvious.

That night, Nejla shared Gulden's bedroom.

'Gulden,' she said hesitantly, 'you seem different from when I saw you at home, at Grandfather's funeral. Please don't misunderstand me, but you seemed – well – frightened and unsure of yourself, like you were under a curse or something. Now you seem, I don't know how to say it, but it's as if you've been freed from something.'

Gulden smiled and nodded with approval as if in agreement. She stood up, walked across to the window and looked out.

'Nejla, have you ever heard of the Bible?'

'Yes, if you mean the *Injil* with Jesus in it.'

'Well, I have been reading the Bible now for nearly a year, but about six months ago something beautiful happened to me, and as you say yourself I was set free.'

Nejla looked closely at her cousin's face; her eyes, the expression of confidence that seemed so attractive and desirable.

'Tell me more.' Nejla's mind flashed back to the bus and her thoughts about 'If God wills it'.

For several hours Gulden shared her discovery with her cousin. She told Nejla how she had been under a curse and about the fear she had experienced. In the middle of those long nights of sleepless fear, God had become real to her and on one night in particular she had felt all the fear melt away.

She giggled. 'Now sometimes I sleep so well my sisters complain they can't wake me in the morning.'

The next day saw the start of a steady flow of visits to relatives and friends, delivering gifts and drinking endless glasses of tea.

The two weeks seemed to fly by, yet Nejla's overriding memory was Gulden's words about being free inside; about a book that is God's word.

One day, Nejla and Gulden decided to go shopping

together. Nejla's father wanted some tools, her mother cloth and some particular kinds of buttons. As they walked around, Gulden pointed to a bookshop in the main street. She looked a little hesitant, then said, 'I'm not trying to push you, Nejla, or anything like that, but that's where I bought my Bible. You can buy one for yourself if you would like to.'

Nejla smiled. 'Oh Gulden, I would love to have a Bible of my own.'

Inside the bookshop there were people buying newspapers, novels and study books. In the corner on a high shelf was a Bible. Nejla reached out and took it. Even as she held it in her hands, a sense of respect for this holy book filled her heart.

In the next few days Nejla spent every spare moment reading her new book. The bus ride home was nearly seventeen hours, but she used every one of those hours to search for God in His holy Bible. She marvelled at the beauty of the writings. She was in awe of the prophet Jesus, and the wisdom and kindness of every word He spoke. She felt a surge of importance when she realised that women, as well as men, were chosen by God. Every so often she would hold the book to herself, look out of the window of the bus, and feel a warmth inside her. Yes, this was what 'If God wills it' was all about; a God who loves and cares for people, a God who loved and personally cared for her, Nejla. She looked around the bus. Some people were sleeping, some eating, almost every adult was smoking, and yet within her heart something danced for joy.

Her sister, Leila, was waiting for her at the bus

station. They hugged each other, and then walked slowly home. Carrying her case between them, they laughed and chattered eagerly. It was good to catch up on each other's news. The first glimpse of her home stirred her deeply. This had been her first time away, and she ran eagerly up the hill to see her mother and father.

It had all been rather wonderful until she had mentioned the holy book.

'You have seen that book?' her father had asked, with suppressed annoyance.

'Oh yes, Father. I was able to spend a lot of time reading it. It is beautifully written and makes me feel nearer to God.'

'What! You have *read* that book? It is against our religion and teaches much evil.'

'Oh no, Father. It is good and teaches purity and loving-kindness . . .'

Grabbing a stick that rested against the wall, her father, in a rage, had hit her repeatedly across the shoulders, back and legs. Would it never end? His anger had confused and grieved her.

Nejla lay still on her bed staring sadly at the ceiling. Her body still ached, yet the precious memories of her times with Gulden and the reading of her new-found treasure, the Bible, comforted her greatly. Then a sudden burst of fear shot through her; her father did not know that she actually had the Bible in her possession.

Quietly she got up, and as quickly as possible, her body aching, she dressed. Taking the book from her case, she carefully wrapped it, hid it under her shawl and crept past Leila's bed.

Slipping quietly and hesitantly down the stairs in case they creaked, she left the house and headed for the grove of trees down the hill. She had always loved that place and one tree in particular. It was twisted and gnarled with age and there was a small hollow in it where she had often hidden her girlish treasures. It was to this tree that she now entrusted her book. After hiding it safely she turned and hurried back to the house, fearful that if her father saw her, he might suspect something. Reaching the house, she went in quietly.

Later, at breakfast, her father acted as if she were not present. 'It is time we got Nejla a husband. It is because she is not properly occupied that she has been able to fill her mind with foolish thoughts. A husband will soon resolve that.'

Gathering courage some days later, Nejla went to the grove of trees. She sat quietly for a while watching the squirrels playing in the grass. Then, hesitantly, she prayed. 'God, I know You are there. Please teach me the truth.'

After a few moments she took her book from its hiding-place and began to read.

'Let not your heart be troubled: you believe in God, believe also in me.'

A leaf fell from the tree as if in slow motion; twisting, turning, and tumbling on its way to the ground. Nejla loved this time of year. It was still warm enough to be comfortable outside as the changing season began to unfold before one's eyes. The deep heavenly green of the leaves began to give

way to yellows, golds, bronze, scarlet, rust, and
oranges that showed another summer had passed.
The squirrels busily hurried to and fro preparing for
the long winter's siege. Despite the tranquillity of the
moment, an awareness of change gave a sense of
activity to the atmosphere.

How she loved this place, Nejla thought to herself.
Fond memories of childhood flooded her mind as she
looked back and remembered the first time she had
seen a squirrel dart in and out of the trees. Being in
this place provided for her a time of innocence, and
isolation from the day to day responsibilities of just
being alive.

This morning, the atmosphere within her little
clump of trees was more intense. The leaves seemed to
glow and sparkle with vibrant, joyful colours, and
that inner sense of rightness that was so new to her
became even more meaningful here.

This little clump of trees, which people passed by
day after day, was to Nejla like a gateway to heaven.
The way that it stood so fresh and clear amidst the
scratchy grey and brown hillside made it stand out
like an oasis. How she loved to be surrounded by
nature; to hear the gentle song of the early morning
birds, or glimpse the scampering field mice that one
could see occasionally by staying very still for a long
time!

She sat down and crossed her legs. Another leaf fell
from a branch and started its slow but definite downward journey. For a moment it was caught by a gentle
breeze, which gave it an added second or two of
suspension, freely gliding before eventually landing in
an almost predetermined position on the ground.

Reaching out to a stalk of grass, Nejla could see her own home in the distance. What a difference between there and here, she thought to herself. Chewing the grass gave her a sense of freedom from the responsibility of growing up. Looking towards the lazy sun with her eyes closed, she could feel the intensity of the light. A warm glow seemed to flow through her, and she felt as though she had been caught up into heaven, into God's presence. Warmth, freshness and safety; the very thought thrilled her heart. She looked down to the patch of grass where she was sitting. A little furry insect, about one inch long, was slowly making its pilgrimage to somewhere over a long branch that had fallen down. Laboriously it marched on. For a moment she was tempted to help it on its way but hesitated to infringe on its dignity. She laughed as she saw her own thoughts becoming so deep, insects with dignity going on pilgrimages! She leaned back against her favourite tree, closed her eyes, chewed the stalk of grass, and decided she was very happy to be alive.

'Nejla! Nejla!'

The sound of her name being called broke the solitude and quietness of her haven like a sudden bolt of thunder tearing across a clear sky.

'Nejla, you'll never guess who is at the house! It's Hamid!'

Her sister, Leila, was panting because she had run from the house without stopping. Breathing heavily and leaning against a tree, Leila went on, 'Father is angry because you are not at home.' She stood upright, pushed out her stomach, arching her back, and in a gruff voice imitated her father. 'She's too old to be out playing on her own, her place is here working in the home.'

Nejla's little world was shattered.

'Do you mean Hamid Rifat?'

'Yes, he is with his elder brother, and his mother and father. Have you ever seen his mother? Just being near her scares me.'

Nejla rose slowly from the ground. Taking the piece of grass out of her mouth and dropping it to the ground seemed to be a symbolic gesture. The day she had dreaded had come.

A large cloud slowly moved across in front of the sun just as another leaf started its downward path. It was almost as if nature itself were making a prophetic statement about Nejla's life.

# 2

# The Rifats

The little pathway leading from the clump of trees up to Nejla's home was usually a joy to walk along. Yet now, as she thought of what tomorrow might hold, a sense of foreboding overshadowed her. A butterfly fluttered by. She stopped and smiled, but this temporary delight could not lighten any of the darkness that seemed to descend even as she walked.

'Where on earth have you been? Your father is going mad with rage.' Nejla's mother looked nervously at her elder daughter. Years of being married to her husband had taught her that he was a man who was impulsive and unpredictable. Many times she had taken a beating from him herself. She was a woman somewhat typical of her age and upbringing; a nervous woman with much creative potential that never had been nor ever would be expressed. She looked out of the kitchen window into the garden. Someone close by had lit a fire and was burning some rubbish. The smoke wafted across into their garden, a black cloud hanging low across the grass.

'I was down by my trees, Mama. You know I love to go there.'

Nejla's face was innocent, but at this moment it showed strain. The uneasy atmosphere intensified as her mother hurriedly helped her into a new dress.

'Well, you shouldn't have been down there. Hamid Rifat is here and the men are working out the dowry arrangement for your wedding. Your father wants you to go in and serve tea to them all.'

Leila was standing in the corner, observing all that was going on. In one way she envied her sister being the centre of attraction. Her mother's commands brought her mind to attention.

'Leila, do something useful. Go and get the cologne from my top drawer.' Then, pushing Nejla into a chair, she began to work on her daughter's long, glossy, raven-black hair.

For some reason, thoughts of the kitchen passed through Nejla's mind. To her, the kitchen was home. As far back as she could remember, the little bottle gas cooker had been in the same place in the corner. The one large table where everyone ate together (except when visitors came) was worn and knotty. The top end nearest the cooker was used for cutting vegetables and meat and even though they always washed it off with a cloth, the years of wear had stained it. She remembered when she had fallen off the table and hit her forehead on the sink and lain still on the ground, and how everyone had thought she was dead. Death – could that be any different from being forced to enter a marriage with someone she did not love?

'Mama, I don't want to get married. I am too young. I feel like it's – well – almost wrong. Can't we wait another year?'

Her mother spoke between the hairclips clenched in her mouth; 'Don't be silly, of course you're not too young, you can marry and have children in no time at all.'

'But that's just it!' Nejla tried to jump up and turn to face her mother but was firmly pushed down as her mother went on preparing her hair.

'Besides, I don't know how to have babies, no one has ever told me. Oh, Mama, I'm scared!' For a moment there was silence as the mother-cum-hairdresser stood back and observed her handiwork.

'Everything will work out just fine. I'll tell you all about it the day before you get married. Where is Leila with that cologne?'

The sense of overwhelming uncertainty created a feeling of panic within Nejla. She thought of her trees and the falling leaves with a sense of futility; perhaps she was just like a leaf falling by some divine fate to a set destination? She tried to recall the dreamy peace that had filled her such a short time before as she sat in the sun, but all she could muster in her mind was the cold vision of the sun being overwhelmed by the large grey cloud. A chill ran up her arms as she thought again of that leaf, falling helplessly, tossed for a moment in the wind as it was carried on its downward pathway.


Mr Rifat was a well-built man with a strong face. His eyes revealed a special, almost spiritual depth. He had worked hard for many years to build his yoghurt business into something that his sons could take over from him. He was known in the community as a friendly, honest man who seemed to bring warmth wherever he went. Now as he sat watching his wife and two sons, his mind wandered back over the years of leading this small family. He looked at Hussein, his elder son; so harsh, bitter and violent. He remembered when Hussein was a small child and how sensitive he had been. One time, when Hamid had brought home a little insect in a matchbox, Hussein had been very upset when Hamid had said the insect was probably a father and had children. He had made Hamid take the insect back to the woods. Yet that same sensitive boy was now a hardened, callous man, separated from his wife just a few days after the wedding.

He looked at Hamid, his other son. How handsome he was, yet so weak-willed, so easily swayed!

Looking at his wife, he sighed. How harsh she had become! Perhaps she had always been severe, he thought to himself. He could not believe that one person could be so consumed with hatred and jealousy.

Often he had wondered if the evening when she went to put a curse on her sister had been the turning point. Not so much the curse itself, for they had been surrounded by such activity all their lives. No, that evening had been different. A wizened old woman who seemed to have strange evil powers came and spent time in the back room preparing a curse. Perhaps the curse had turned on itself, and that was why his wife was so full of hatred.

Nejla's father sat on the other side of the room. He was an enormous man. His eyes were a little wild and he seemed to have a three-day-old beard. He shouted rather than spoke. His accent was not from that region, which added even more to the differences between him and Mr Rifat.

In the kitchen Nejla continued to prepare for her encounter with the Rifat family. She seemed, for a moment, detached from what was going on. Her mother was primping her hair, preparing her like some prize animal for the market. Leila finally appeared with the cologne. Nejla's mind had been wandering to thoughts of the city, her childhood, and her Bible.

Nejla's dream world was shattered as her mother spoke. 'Okay, you are ready to go in. Remember, don't say anything, don't look Hamid's brother in the eyes, and smile at his mother.'

Trembling with fear, Nejla looked even more innocent and attractive as she walked into the sitting-room to serve tea.

# 3

# *Chosen*

Hussein's fist smashed against the wall with a mighty force. He cried out in pain and then slumped up against the wall with his forehead touching the rough plaster.

'Oh God, they're all poison! Poison!' he whispered, with violence and precision.

His body slid down the wall and he sat in a heap on the floor, temporarily relieved from the tension that had built up within himself. Why had his life turned bitter so soon? he asked himself.

From where he sat he could see the clock on the shelf in the far corner of the room. A large crack had spread across the outer glass. He remembered the evening when his mother had first told him that his wife was cheap and unfaithful, and how he had screamed in anger and thrust his hand out and smashed that clock, the nearest thing in reach. He thought of his own home and how his mother, slowly and over the years, had begun to dominate his father.

'Women – they are all filth!' he spat out, still sitting
on the floor and aware by now that his hand was
hurting.

The door opened and Hamid appeared in the
archway, a look of surprise on his face.

'Goodness, what on earth has happened?' Hamid
was shocked to see his brother in such an agitated
state of mind.

Hussein, still nursing his fist, lifted himself off the
floor and into an armchair.

'Hey, what's wrong?' Hamid looked concerned.

Hussein looked the picture of despair. His head lay
back on the chair. He looked numbly at the ceiling. A
cigarette hung limply from his lips. A trail of smoke,
floating directly upwards, was interrupted in its
journey only by his sporadic breathing.

'I don't understand what is wrong with you these
days.' Hamid raised his hands appealingly.

'What's wrong? What's wrong? Look at what's
happening!'

Hussein jerked forward and flicked his cigarette
into the fire.

'First it's my life, destroyed by the poison of
women's lies, and now you are happily moving into
the battlefield to be torn apart by their claws.'

'Oh, come on, you can't say that about Nejla.
You've seen her; she is soft, gentle and sweet.'

Hussein turned and looked squarely into Hamid's
face. 'And Mama, what about her?'

Hamid, taken aback by the violence of his
brother's words, physically stepped back. He looked
at the ground, and, as though frozen, could not
answer. The moment of intensity passed and Hamid

said, 'Okay, Hussein, let me tell you this straight. Your marriage did not work because the girl was bad. That is not the case with me. So let's make things clear; I am going to marry Nejla and I don't care what you say or think.'

Hussein looked across the room back to the clock with the broken glass. He felt anger rise within him, yet forcibly controlled his desire to hit Hamid. 'The fool, the utter fool!' he whispered as he deliberately turned his back upon his brother. Didn't he realise the sweeter they looked, the more deceptive and wicked they were?

Nejla sat alone in her room. Earlier she had spoken to her father.

'Father, I don't want to marry Hamid.'

'What? Since when have I allowed you to have what you want?' A wild look of anger filled his eyes.

'Father, you don't understand. I love God and I can't marry a man who doesn't share my faith.'

'Can't?' Her father's face flushed with rage. 'If I say you are to marry, then you will marry and your silly likes and dislikes will be forgotten.'

'Please, Father!' Nejla pleaded, her eyes moist with tears.

'Don't argue with me,' her father shouted and grabbed a belt from the hook on the wall. As the belt flashed overhead, raining blows on her back and shoulders, he shouted abuse at her. When his anger had cooled off slightly, Nejla lay huddled in the corner, weeping as though her heart would break. Then, looking up through tear-filled eyes, past hair that had fallen like a veil over her face, she whispered, through her sobs, 'I love you, Father.'

The unexpected reply brought a feeling of almost guilt and unease to Nejla's father. Abruptly he turned and stamped towards the door. Pausing, he shouted over his shoulder before he slammed the door, 'You'll marry whoever I choose and there will be no more arguments!'

On her bed lay her soft teddy bear. Picking it up, she remembered how as a child she had always cuddled that little bear whenever she was sad or lonely. Now as she hugged her little friend she began to cry; at first gently but then, as she dropped to her knees, she sobbed as though her heart would break. Why was this happening and why just now? As her sobs subsided she began to pray. 'Oh Lord, why does this have to happen to me? Why do I have to go through with this? Oh please Lord, don't let it happen to me. He doesn't love You and I had so longed to be able to pray with my husband. Oh, what shall I do?'

Just being able to be honest with God helped. Climbing onto her bed, her little woollen bear close to her face, merciful sleep engulfed her.


Hamid took the short cut that led him down a steep bank, arriving at a dimly lit cobblestone street.

He felt quite exhilarated. This Nejla was not the usual type. Being with her, although briefly, he had sensed that she was different. There was a quality of character about her that was quite distinctive.

Entering the tea house, he was greeted by a loud

cheer. All his friends had heard about the meeting
that afternoon. He felt a flush rising up his neck,
laughed, and then bowed. Everyone clapped,
stamped and cheered. Somehow this attention made
him feel special.

The crowded tea house buzzed with an
unexplainable electric atmosphere. There was a radio
in the corner blaring music. At each table it seemed as
if some unique activity was going on. In the corner
two men were shouting at each other, next to them
two others were playing backgammon as if those
shouting did not exist. On the wall was a picture of a
man dressed up as a woman. Hamid looked at the
picture. 'How could that be a man?' he thought to
himself, then laughed and turned his attention to the
backgammon game.

This was home, he thought to himself, to be here
was really a part of his own identity; to be rejected by
these his friends would be the greatest of all tragedies
that could ever befall him. His forthcoming marriage
created a new acceptance for him here in this place.
How he needed it! he thought to himself.

# 4

# *Sold*

The sunlight filtering through a gap in the curtain in Nejla's bedroom seemed to be carrying a message of hope as it tumbled into her life. Though uninvited, it was nevertheless a welcome visitor in the middle of her sorrow. Feeling the sun on her face took her mind back to the hillside when, just a few days ago, she had imagined looking up to the throne of God.

Looking to one side, she saw Leila deep in slumber. Leila looked so beautiful, so restful. Nejla couldn't help thinking what beautiful eyebrows her younger sister had as she lay there looking so peaceful. Yet even this brought her a certain amount of pain as she thought of Leila having to face marriage in just a few years. How she wished there was some way to capture their childhood and hold all their problems at bay!

She still had not accepted the fact that she had to marry Hamid. As she obeyed her parents, was it possible that she could genuinely begin to love

Hamid? That she could go through with the marriage and actually find any kind of joy?

Suddenly the section of the Bible she had read the day before came to her mind. 'In all things give thanks.' She couldn't remember where it was found but she definitely remembered reading it. At the time it had not really made an impression but now it seemed to burst with meaning for her situation. What a test to her faith; to actually be thankful to God for her possible marriage to Hamid! At first, the thought made her shudder. Then instinctively she got up from her bed, walked across to the window and looked out. In the distance she could see her clump of trees. She could give thanks for the trees, they had special meaning. But to give thanks for Hamid and their coming marriage – that seemed impossible.

After an inward struggle, as a conscious act of obedience, she took a deep breath, held it for a second and then whispered so as not to waken Leila, 'I don't feel like giving thanks but, oh God, I thank You for allowing this situation to happen and I trust You with my life.' At that point an overwhelming sense of peace began to flood through her heart. She was filled with a sense of calm, with a gentle awareness that God was involved with her life, and that she was cared for and loved.

Leila began to stir, rubbed her eyes, then turning over, caught sight of Nejla, who was still by the window. How she loved her sister! she thought to herself. She was so kind, so gentle, and so real. Leila decided that real was probably the best word to describe her. She thought back to last week when she had told Nejla, 'I wish I was like you.' The words of comfort and wisdom that followed made her love her even more. 'You are you, Leila, and you are special just as you are. I love you and accept you because you are yourself.' Even as she thought back, a surge of warmth seemed to spring up inside her. 'Oh Nejla,' she said in the whisper of thought, 'I do love you. I hope Hamid will make you happy.'

As Hussein lit another cigarette, he thought of the newspaper article he had recently read about a man who fell asleep while smoking. The house had burnt down. 'Who cares?' he began to think. 'So what if we die? Life is a burden. Pleasure is the only thing worth looking for, love only brings bitterness.

'Love is cruel. Love, what is love anyway? Just an imaginary game that we are sold in the market-place of our minds by these foolish romantic films, books and magazines.'

Lying there he thought of Nejla, wondering how long the marriage would last between her and his brother. She was pretty, his brother was right, and there was something different about her from the other girls he knew.

Nejla's father burst through the door, half shouting in his excitement. 'It's fixed! It's fixed!' He genuinely looked happy, although perhaps relief would be a better way of describing his feelings. He was relieved that this daughter who was a potential problem because of her religious beliefs was now going to be married. He laughed loudly as if he was almost going to lose control of himself.

'The date, have you set a date?' Nejla's mother enquired anxiously as she hurried into the room.

He took a long drink from a glass of orange juice. The action seemed to intensify the suspense. Looking up, he replied with an air of superiority, 'Of course, what do you think I've been doing all this time?'

'When is it?' Leila and her mother spoke together. The father enjoyed his sense of being master of their suspense and dragged his act out even further.

'Oh Daddy, when?' cried Leila indignantly.

'Saturday,' he answered casually.

'Saturday!' they both screamed. 'That's only four days away. You're crazy. There will never be time to prepare.' Rarely had his wife shown such courage before him, and he was quite taken aback.

'It's all to do with taxes and the arrangement.'

'What arrangement?' his wife shouted.

'The arrangement. And don't act so high and mighty with me. When I speak, it is law. The arrangement concerns Leila's marriage.'

There was a sudden stillness that was electric. His wife gasped, as if panting for air, 'To whom?'

'Hamid's elder brother, of course. She will marry on her fifteenth birthday.'

Leila looked with anguish first at her father and then at her mother, who had collapsed with shock into the nearest chair. In despair, she ran from the room.

'How, how could you?' her mother whispered. 'He is divorced and has a horrible scandal around his last marriage. Besides, she is just a child. How could you marry her to such a hardened man? You did this just to gain financially on the dowry arrangements, didn't you? Don't you even care about your daughter's happiness?'

'Enough!' His words cut like a knife. 'You women are like children, totally incapable of making important decisions. We men look ahead to the future and don't base important decisions on silly emotional female ideas. I don't ever want to hear you speak to me like this again.'

Nejla's father stormed out of the house, and kicked at (but missed) the cat sitting near the front gate. He would go to the tea house with the men; anyway, what did these women know? They were just like children.

Nejla had been working in the vegetable patch and hadn't heard the storm going on in the house. Going inside to help prepare lunch, Nejla found her mother weeping brokenly. 'Mother dear, what has happened?' She put her arms tenderly around her mother.

'It's your father. You're to be married in four days. And Leila, my baby, is to be married to Hussein when she is fifteen,' she sobbed.

A wave of nausea swept over Nejla and for a moment she felt as if she would faint. Horrified, she cried, 'No, he won't do such a wicked thing to Leila. She is his beloved daughter. He would never marry her to Hussein.'

'Oh Nejla, to lose you both so suddenly! And what if Hamid is like his brother? What if you are hurt? It's unthinkable to marry both my daughters into the same family, and surely it is inevitable that Leila will be hurt. Oh, what can we do?'

'Mama,' Nejla spoke hesitantly, 'Mama, perhaps if

we ask Jesus, He will help us. He says, "Come unto Me, all you who are heavy-hearted". I know He loves us and He hears if we call on Him.'

'Nejla, He is not the one we were taught to pray to. You should not speak about Him. Besides, even if He is real, He wouldn't care about women and their heartaches. No, you pray if you like but I just can't.'

Disappointed, Nejla went slowly up the stairs. Only four days and she would be married! She had always looked on marriage as something in the future but now it was just a matter of hours away. Had God heard her prayers? Was her mother right that He would not concern Himself with her heartaches because she was a girl? She had believed God would save her from this marriage. Now to make things worse, her beloved little sister was to be married to a man with a bad reputation. If God loved them, how could He allow both of them to be forced into a loveless marriage?

Leila lay on her bed silent, almost deathlike, staring at the ceiling. The sparkle and exuberance that were so characteristic of her were gone, and she seemed to have suddenly aged.

A wave of pity flooded Nejla's heart as she saw her. All thoughts of herself were pushed away as she ran to her sister's side.

'Oh Leila, poor sweet Leila.'

'I have been sold. I thought Father loved me but he has sold me, taking no more thought for my happiness than he would over a sheep he was selling to the highest bidder.'

'Oh no, Leila, I'm sure he meant well. He probably

thought it would be nice for us to marry brothers. That way we can look after each other.'

'You know he always loves to look for a good deal, a deal where he feels he's got the best. That's all we are to him, a business arrangement. I hate him.'

Nejla sat on the bed beside Leila, praying silently for some way of comforting her sister.

'I think I shall end my life,' Leila said carelessly.

'Oh no, Leila. Life is a precious gift from God. You can't be serious.'

'No? To marry Hussein is worse than death. It would be an act of truth to end my life. Besides, all my hopes have been smashed and one just can't live without hope. There would be no meaning to my existence.'

'But there *is* hope. Remember I told you that the Lord is like a shepherd who really loves and protects His sheep? Well, if you ask Him into your life, He will take care of you. He will be your reason for living, His love will enfold you. He will never betray you or leave you. His desire will be to share all your sorrow and to bring you a sense of peace and joy that no one can take away from you.'

'Do you really believe God is interested in our problems?'

'Yes, yes I do. He's not only interested, but He works for us to change things that we can't bear. He says, "Ask and it shall be given to you, that your joy may be full." He wants to do good to us, never evil. The Lord loves you, Leila, but you must open your heart to Him.'

'No! When someone opens their heart, they only get hurt. I don't think I can ever trust a man again,

*Nejla*

not even your Lord, Nejla.' Leila began to weep. 'Nejla, I'm scared. Help me, please help me, I'm so scared.'

Quickly Nejla's arms went around her sister, drawing her close and gently rocking her as she would a small child. Tears stung her eyes at the thought of the unfairness of the whole situation. Praise the Lord in everything? How could she ever praise Him for this?

Supper time was tense, with mother and daughters merely pushing their food around their plates while their father ate with an air of celebration.

Both girls went to bed early. Leila, cuddling the teddy bear, longing to recapture the unawareness of childhood, yet feeling her heart gripped with despair, began to think of death.

'I would rather die than face this, it is just too much to bear,' were her last thoughts as she drifted into an uneasy sleep.

Nejla, unable to sleep, slipped out of bed, and went to the window. The garden was bathed in moonlight and looked so fresh and lovely. She longed to go down to her trees but knew her father would not approve. The light of the moon was sparkling on the leaves of the tree near her window. 'It is strange that there can be beauty so close to me when my heart is so heavy,' she thought. Tears began to fall down her cheeks. 'Oh Lord, do You care? Do You see the injustice that goes on here? You say give thanks in everything. Even in the middle of an injustice? Even when your heart is breaking? Do You know what it is like to be sold? To be hurt — betrayed by the one You love? Can You understand what it's like to be at the mercy of others who really only want to please themselves?'

In the quietness, it seemed that a gentle voice spoke. 'I was sold for thirty pieces of silver by one who was My friend, whom I loved. Then people I had made took Me, and beat Me, cursed and spat upon Me, and then hung Me on a tree. My heart was broken because of My love for you as your sins were placed on Me. I see your hurt but I want you to forgive your father and I want you to praise Me for this situation.'

Falling to her knees, weeping, Nejla prayed. 'Oh Lord, forgive me. Thank You for allowing Yourself to be hurt. You took that path because You love me. I love You so much. Your comfort is real because You triumphed over pain. Thank You. Help me to forgive my father and accept this situation as from Your loving hand. Forgive me for my resentment. Help me to be willing to love Hamid. I know I will only be able to love him as You fill my heart with Your love. Oh Lord, help me love him, help me love him with Your love.'

# 5

# *The news*

Hamid's father sat in his favourite chair. He looked out of the window that backed onto the woods. In his hand he held a glass of tea. He hummed softly to the music playing; it was his favourite, folk-dance music from the mountains. He thought back to his own child-hood in the mountains; the weddings, the celebrations at circumcision, the drums, the *saz* playing its lively chords. He thought of his own father, such a magnificent man, and of the days when they had gone hunting together. As he thought of these things, sadness filled his heart as he considered his own sons.

His thoughts were interrupted as Hamid walked into the room. Hamid always seemed to look the same, smart and clever yet lost, like a cork bobbing about on a lake.

'Hamid, sit down, son. I've got something to tell you.'

Hamid loved his father yet felt a greater sense of duty to his mother.

'Hamid, you realise that I have not been well recently, don't you?'

Hamid nodded, wondering what his father was going to say.

'Well, I am actually very unwell.' He hesitated, then turned and looked out of the window. 'The doctors have told me that I do not have long to live.'

Hamid gasped, 'Papa, what do you mean?'

His father continued, 'It's okay. We are all given a time to die, it is written. My only regret is that I will not die a happy or a fulfilled man.' He turned to face his son. By now the sun had begun to sink behind the trees. There was a deep interweaving of pastel colours in the sky.

'I wish I knew why I feel this emptiness inside.'

Hamid looked at his father, stunned.

'Well, that I cannot change, dying I cannot change. Hamid, I want you and Hussein to keep the business going.' He smiled. 'I know yoghurt is not the richest business to be in, but it's steady and I've built up what we have for nearly thirty years. It can be yours, and your own son's future.

'I've seen this girl you are to marry, she is different, she is a special person. Be sure not to let your mother poison your mind as she did with Hussein.'

Hamid sat motionless. He couldn't speak, he could hardly take in all that was happening. It seemed inconceivable that his father would die. Surely there was some mistake, perhaps the doctors were wrong!

The music continued to play in the background.

Hamid himself had never visited the mountains where his father had grown up. He had heard the stories as a boy of how his father had ridden horses bareback. He remembered the story of his uncle who had been stabbed several times in the stomach and left for dead by robbers. Yet, after two days lying on the floor, he had slowly begun to heal. Then, when he had recovered totally, he had followed the robbers for months on end until finally he found them both and shot them dead.

His father had said the mountain people were tough, men who would kill for honour. Yet it all seemed so distant to him now, the stories of friends that his father used to tell him at bedtime. Now all he could see was a man he loved who would soon be dead. Hamid stood up, left the room, and went to his own room. Standing by the window, he wept.

Hamid's father sank back into his chair and closed his eyes. Why did he have this empty feeling in his life? he asked himself. He pushed his mind back to his childhood, the horses, the family, his father. He remembered his circumcision well; he was eleven years old, he remembered the way he had screamed when he was cut and how the men had laughed as he screamed. He smiled, then drifted into sleep.

# 6

# *Leila's prayer*

Holding hands, the two sisters strolled down the little
path that led to the stream just behind their house.
The sunlight and warmth of the day seemed to create
an atmosphere of security, despite the sense of
impending doom that hung over them as they walked.

'Leila, I love you dearly. I love Mama and Father,
in spite of what is happening, but I love you in a
special way.' Nejla squeezed her sister's hand as she
spoke. 'I know Mama and Father love you too. You
know, God can help us even in the middle of this
crisis.' She smiled as she turned to Leila.

'Nejla, please don't misunderstand me. I think this
faith you have is good, but I'm so bitter I can't think
of anything else apart from running away or killing
myself.' Leila's voice showed a determination far
beyond her years. 'I know they love us but I feel like
we are cattle or sheep that are being sold off.'

The stream at this time of the year was quite low.
As it bubbled along its way, it seemed a picture of

purity and life. As the two sisters sat down, a frog jumped across into the water from the other side. At any other time this would have drawn squeals of delight from them.

Nejla had to some degree come to terms with the future for herself. She trusted in God. She was more concerned for Leila; thoughts of her sister occupied her mind constantly and weighed heavily upon her.

Leila's words of running away or killing herself also worried her. Leila was impulsive and might put her ideas into action.

'Can we pray together?' Nejla asked.

'If you want,' Leila replied, more to please her sister than because of any personal conviction.

'Lord,' Nejla bowed her head, an aura of peace radiating from her, 'we ask You to help us in our situation. Please either give Leila the same peace You have given me, or else please stop her wedding from taking place.'

At this, Leila shook her sister. 'Do you really think that God would stop my wedding?'

'He can,' Nejla replied, a little shocked at being shaken mid-prayer, 'but it doesn't mean He will, especially if it's His plan for your life.'

'I am going to pray.' Leila suddenly bowed her head. 'Oh God, please stop my wedding and I will be a follower like Nejla.'

'Oh Leila, you can't pray like that.'

'Well, I just have, and I feel better. Let's go back home, Mother will need help.'

Nejla wasn't quite sure what she had started but at least Leila had prayed in faith.

The tiny cobblestone street turned sharply and suddenly became steep. It had been raining; a drizzly light rain, which left an atmosphere of greyness all around. The light that filtered through from the grey cloudy sky made the cobblestones shine very slightly. The steps that ran up and down the side of the street were muddy from the dirty water running off the hill.

However, for Nejla, sunshine shone in her heart. The grey cloudy day had no dampening impression on the intense joy and sense of purpose she was experiencing. Going to the market had always been one of her great joys as a younger girl. Today though, there was also an expectancy for the future. God would answer her prayers. How, she did not know, but she was confident that God would make no mistake. And so, the future held further opportunities to prove God's love in such a difficult situation.

As she turned the corner, she jumped with surprise. 'What are you doing out here alone?' hissed Hamid's mother, who had appeared from nowhere. Her vicious haggard face came close to Nejla's soft olive skin. She looked deeply into Nejla's eyes. 'Answer me, what are you doing here alone?'

Nejla, taken aback, was momentarily frozen to the spot. 'I was going to the market. I always do on Thursdays.'

'I know about you, Nejla, I've seen you talking with those young men down at the tea house. You were going to meet someone, weren't you?'

'No, that's not true!'

Saliva spat from the old woman's lips as she spoke. 'My son is too good for you. If you come and live in my house, you will do what I tell you. You will be

*Nejla*

obedient to me. If I ever see you with any men again, I will have a curse put on you that will make you die a slow and horrible death.'

Before Nejla could reply, the old woman had gone. Nejla collapsed against the wall of a house, feeling both faint and sick. She had not been talking with any of the young men, so why had Hamid's mother spoken so harshly to her?

She looked down at the cobblestones. The rain had stopped and they were beginning to dry out. The slight sheen had vanished. For a moment she thought the sunshine in her heart would vanish too.

Looking down the hill, she could see how far she had walked. It had been hard work but she had made it. Perhaps that new chapter of her life would be the same; hard, like walking up a slippery cobblestone hill. Yet she would make it. By God's grace and with His help, she would not only survive but experience joy in her heart.

The room was so full, it was uncomfortable. A bowl of peanuts had been knocked over and the nuts were mingled with the cigarette ends that had also inadvertently found their way onto the floor. Just below the ceiling hung a fog of heat and cigarette smoke, over a mass of bobbing, laughing, arguing, talking heads.

Nejla was the topic of conversation on everyone's lips. Her raven hair shone, side ringlets gave her an almost royal appearance. Her face, a light olive tone, flushed from the heat, reflected an inner beauty that was totally at peace in the midst of all the noise and confusion. Her large brown eyes blinked occasionally in a natural girlish way. Her lips, perfectly proportioned, with just a hint of make-up, made an ideal setting for her ivory white teeth. The little dimple on her chin seemed more prominent. Almost without exception, all in the room saw this young woman as a very beautiful person and also sensed a depth of character that was attractive. The exception was Hamid's mother, who hovered around some of the older women in the room. Their talk centred on whether Nejla would bear children quickly and if she could produce males. Also, what was the significance of the dimple, did it signify a happy life for her first-born? It was the usual chatter of such women.

Hamid looked proud; proud of himself for the way he looked and proud of the fact he had such a beautiful bride to set off his good looks.

In the far corner, Hussein sat alone smoking a cigarette. He was watching Leila help serve the food and drinks. She, aware of his gaze upon her, busied herself and tried not to be too obvious in her rejection of him.

Nejla's mother was crying and saying how beautiful her young daughter looked. She would be such a good wife. Nejla's father was in the centre of the room talking and laughing loudly with a group of men.

There was another world carried on at knee level in the room. This was the world of the little people darting in and out, full of mischief, happily chasing each other. Occasionally one of them would thump too hard in his excitement and make an adult spill a drink or drop some food.

All through the evening, Nejla's mother wiped tears from her eyes. They were tears of relief that somehow in four days the wedding had been arranged; tears at the thought of losing her gracious daughter, and tears of joy at the romantic thoughts of marriage and happiness she desired for her. She had often looked forward to the day when her daughters would marry. But this had been so sudden; 'I will be sorry to see Leila go but at least I have six months to prepare for her wedding,' she thought to herself, as conversation buzzed around her.

'The stars are beautiful, Hamid,' Nejla said shyly. At last they were alone. Just being away from the noise gave a sense of relief to both of them, and yet Nejla felt nervous.

'They are clear tonight, and the air is so fresh.' Hamid put his arm possessively around her shoulders as he spoke, and thought how soft and beautiful her hair was.

'Hamid,' Nejla said softly and hesitantly, 'Hamid, I want to be a good wife, to make you happy.'

Hamid felt a sensation of warmth rise up from his stomach and fill his chest as he gazed into her face.

'Nejla, you are beautiful.'

As they walked back to Hamid's home, they could hear the sound of a night owl. Nejla prayed a silent prayer to her God, 'Lord, thank You that You are with me wherever I go. Help me to be the kind of woman who reflects Your love. Teach me to love this man and to keep praising You no matter what happens in the days to come.'

# 7

# *Without Nejla*

The room was silent except for the sound of rain
dripping off the roof and pattering against the
window. Leila glanced about her, feeling like an
actress in a play. Lying on her bed was the teddy bear
that by now had become a symbol of both Nejla's and
her own innocence. Nejla's bed lay empty. The sheets
and pillows had been removed and just the bare
mattress remained. At the lower end of the mattress
was a stain where coffee had been spilt. The bed
looked desolate; so detached from the memories that
Leila had of her beloved sister. She thought back to
the times when she used to wake in the middle of the
night and find comfort just by Nejla being near.

Looking out of the window she could see the little
clump of trees that meant so much to her sister. The
rain made them seem distant, almost unreal;
somewhat like Leila's own feelings at the moment,
almost as if she were in a dream.

Looking down at the bottle in her hands, she

calmly wondered if the pills would kill her or if she would just be terribly ill. It wasn't as if her feelings were intense or reckless, or that she wanted to end her life in one crushing moment of despair. Rather she felt tired inside. The heaviness she felt oppressed her and made her feel that it was more of a burden to live than to die.

On the table was a glass of water. Mechanically she reached out to it and held it, as she slowly began to pour the pills from the bottle onto the table.

The sound of water on the window seemed to grow louder and a thrill seized Leila, as she realised that the end of her life was just moments away.

Picking up a handful of the pills, she slowly opened her mouth. Carefully putting the pills into her mouth, she raised the glass of water to her lips. Over the rim of the glass she could see the clump of trees and in her mind she remembered the day she and Nejla had walked and prayed together. Just two days later, Nejla was married and now she herself was going to die.

Closing her eyes as if to shut out the memories, she touched the glass to her lips. From far away she heard her sister calling, 'Leila, it's me. Don't swallow them.' With an effort she opened her eyes, and found herself looking into her beloved sister's face. Spitting the pills out, Leila collapsed into Nejla's arms, weeping uncontrollably.

Nejla held her close, and even in the middle of her sobs, Leila thought how warm and safe she felt in her sister's arms.

'Leila, dear, dear Leila. Nothing is so terrible that you need to resort to this.'

The pills lay scattered on the floor and table. The glass had been knocked over and water trickled across the table onto the floor.

Nejla stood up for a moment, reached across and picked up the empty bottle and looked at the label. Pointing towards the pills that lay scattered about, she said, 'These wouldn't have killed you. They would have made your stomach bleed and caused you horrible pain.'

'I can't stand it. I can't stand being alone without you. I can't stand seeing that bed empty. I can't stand the thought of being married to Hussein!'

Taking Leila's hand, Nejla walked across to the window and looked out to the clump of trees. 'Life is a gift God has given to you, Leila. Before you were even born, while you were in Mother's womb, God saw you, loved you, and had a plan for your life. To die, or even to make yourself ill by taking these pills was not part of His plan. Leila, I love you dearly and I wish you could understand how much God wants to be involved in every detail of your life.'

'Oh, Nejla,' Leila reached out and put her arms around her sister. As their cheeks brushed together, the tears that flowed from their eyes mingled, like a sign of the depth of the oneness they had with each other.

Later, as the girls sat downstairs drinking tea, Leila began to talk. 'I suppose it's hard for me to accept that you've gone. I didn't realise I'd be so lonely.'

'But Leila, I haven't really gone. It's not as if I'm even in another town. We can still spend time together; you can come over in the day when Hamid is at work.'

As they talked, Leila began to unwind. Nejla always seemed to be able to make things seem less terrible. Then Leila's eyes happened to fall on the corner where the wedding photographs stood. Could even Nejla make the prospect of marriage to Hussein a lighter burden than it was becoming?

# 8

# *Young Love*

Weeks later Nejla was thinking how good God was. He had answered her prayer and caused the seed of love to begin to grow within her for her husband. She treasured this as a special proof of God's love for her, and experienced a sense of contentment in all she did.

'I can't even begin to tell you how much I love these trees, Hamid.'

Nejla loosed her hand from Hamid's and ran like a little girl around a tree, holding onto the trunk with one hand.

'I don't understand why.' Hamid loved his young bride and felt he was a fortunate man to have someone like her, but didn't fully understand the way she thought.

'It's hard to explain, but see that little squirrel up in the branches of the tree? He is safe and secure, away from danger, free to be alive without the hostility of life on the ground crushing his spirit. That's what these trees mean to me.'

Near the edge of the clump was one old tree that was quite distinctive. It was not really tall but seemed strong and determined, as if at one time it had struggled to survive. It had a trunk that was twisted and gnarled, which gave it a look of character and made it stand out from the rest of the trees.

'Hamid, this is my favourite tree. Whenever I look at it, I feel a sense of hope rising within me.'

Holding hands again, they stood together and looked at the tree. The sun shone warmly on their backs. Little birds flitted in and out of the trees and the fragrances from the various flowers made them both feel very much alive and in love.

'Hamid, let's make this our tree.'

Hamid turned to his young wife and looked deep into her brown eyes, which contained a universe of mystery and yet were practical and kind, and sparkled with life. 'You really want to share everything with me, don't you?'

'Darling,' she put both hands on his face and gently kissed him. 'Everything I have is yours. I lie in bed and think of how I can make you happy the next day.'

Hamid reached out, stroked her cheek gently and then drew her to him. 'Nejla, I love you more than anything in the world.' He kissed her on the lips, then the tip of her nose. They both turned and looked at the tree. Hamid reached out to one of the branches as if it were a person.

'What shall we call it?'

'How about Young Love?'

Hamid looked across to Nejla. 'Young Love. That's beautiful. Now we are young and in love. One day the glow of romance will wear off and then we can look back and remember our young and "in love" days.'

'Oh Hamid, if we trust God then the roots of our love will grow deep and strong just like this tree, so that no matter what storm we face, our love will support us.'

A beautiful butterfly with green and black markings fluttered by. The warmth from the sun gave an almost make-believe atmosphere to the setting. Young Love was more than a tree, it had become a symbol of hope for the love and devotion of two young people.


Hussein sat reading the newspaper, a cup of coffee on the little table by him, a chunk of fresh bread in one hand and a cigarette in the other.

'It's all rubbish. I don't want to hear about it. You feel in love? Great. But it's not for me.'

'You say that, but you wait until you and her sister get together. That will change your mind.'

Hussein took a long draw on his cigarette, then crumpled the newspaper. 'You seem to forget, young lover, I've been through this routine before. They're all bad, you've got to treat them like small children or animals that can't think for themselves. You make them do things that please you and you beat them if they don't please you. The only point of marriage is to have a servant you needn't pay and someone to bear you sons.'

'You don't really mean that.' Hamid looked annoyed at his elder brother's attitude towards love.

Hussein stood up, walked across to the open fire and spat into it. 'I mean it all right, and if this marriage of mine goes through, you will see just how much I mean it. Give them just one inch and they will do you in. Come on, let's face it, look at Mama and Papa. He used to be strong and in control but ever since he's been ill Mama has begun to manipulate him. Well, that's not going to happen to me.'

Hamid seemed confused but listened reluctantly as his brother went on, 'Love? You don't know what you're talking about.'

# 9

# The garden

'What are you reading?' Hamid looked across the softly lit room to Nejla, sitting on the couch. Every day when Hamid returned home from work, as he walked through the door, he was greeted by a lovely aroma. Tonight, candles glowed softly on the table, which was already laid for dinner.

'It's a love story.' Nejla smiled girlishly, unconscious of how irresistible her husband found her.

'A love story! You women are all the same.' Nejla giggled as Hamid reached over, kissed her, and took the book from her hands. 'It's a Bible. Where did you get this from? I've never seen one before, although I have heard of it.'

'It's mine. I've had it for some time, but it's just the last few months that it has become so precious to me. Let me read you something. "I am the rose of Sharon, the lily of the valley. As the lily among thorns, so is my love among the daughters. As the apple tree among the trees of the wood, so is my beloved among the sons. He brought me to the banqueting house, and his banner over me was love. The voice of my beloved! Behold, he comes leaping upon the mountains, skipping upon the hills. My beloved is like a roe or a young hart. My beloved spoke, and said to me, Rise up, my love, my fair one, and come away. For lo, the winter is past, the rain is over and gone; the flowers appear on the earth, and the song of the turtledove is heard in the land.'' '

'That's beautiful. Who are the characters?' The glow of the candles on Nejla's face highlighted her beauty, and Hamid leaned over and kissed her, then sat down beside her.

'It's like this, Hamid; God loves us. His love is very personal. You know, He loves you, and He loves me, each as individuals. When we experience His love, it's like living in a beautiful garden. Even though this world is horrid and people may hurt us or misunderstand us, as we experience God's love in our lives, it is like being safe in His special garden.'

'Well, I've certainly never heard religion explained like that but even so, I'm not sure I like you reading this book.'

'Yes, my master.' Nejla slipped off the couch and bowed down before Hamid. 'But master, my Bible tells me to love you, be kind to you, care for you. Should I forget this and be a wife who . . .'

'Okay, okay, you silly goose, I get the point. You may read your Bible but just make sure you don't talk about it to my family or friends.'

Nejla laughed and rested her head on Hamid's knees. 'Hamid, dear, I know it's hard for you to understand, but it's the message of the Bible that gives me strength to live by. Please don't misunderstand me but it's God who gives me the deep love I have for you.'

She slipped into a sitting position on the floor and slowly undid Hamid's shoes. Then tenderly and firmly she began to massage his feet. Looking up she smiled. 'Hamid, God has shown me that loving you is a way of serving Him.'

The candle on the table flickered and nearly went out, but they hardly noticed, taken up with their love for each other. Hamid reached down to Nejla's face and cupped it in his hands. 'You are incredible, and I love you.'

# 10

# Music

This was the third day running that Nejla had come to her little clump of trees. Being by Young Love, feeling the roughness of its twisted trunk gave her a sense of being close to Hamid, even though she was alone.

This morning was different. It was lovely to be by Young Love, yet she had a heaviness of heart that caused her great pain. Hamid's father had been taken ill in the night and had been rushed to the hospital. She could see now the despair in Hamid's eyes as he had walked up the path with the news that his father might live only a few more days. She had wanted to go with Hamid to be with her father-in-law but Hamid's mother forbade it. Hamid's father had shown much fondness to Nejla and even though they didn't see much of him, when they did he had always seemed glad that they were married. Now he lay dying and she felt helpless, not being allowed to visit him and to tell him how death could be like going into a beautiful garden, if he only would believe.

'Oh Lord, I do so want to be able to see Hamid's father so I can tell him of Your love for him. To share how death can be something beautiful and peaceful for him if he would turn to You.'

Nejla found herself weeping in a deeply spiritual way as she felt the burden of her father-in-law's soul pressing upon her heart. 'Oh Lord, please let me see him.'

Moments later the sound of her name being called cut through the peace of the tiny arbour where she was sitting by her beloved tree. Hamid had known instinctively she would be down by their tree and had come there in search of her.

'You must come with me to the hospital, Papa keeps asking for you.' Hamid was panting as if he had been running some distance.

'But your mother . . .'

'Oh, forget that now! He's asking for you and I want you to go to him.'

The bed, covered with soiled linen, stood in a room that looked quite empty with only a table and chair in the corner. As soon as Nejla walked in she noticed the linen and thought that she must bring some fresh sheets. She was shocked by the sight of her father-in-law who, pale and deathlike, lay with his mouth open, breathing in short sporadic gasps like an injured animal.

She reached over and held his hand in her own and kissed it. Slowly he moved his head in her direction. 'Nejla,' he mouthed, but no sound came out. He spoke again and it seemed as if it took all his energy just to gasp her name.

As she looked at her father-in-law, whom she had grown to love, a great surge of compassion flooded through her. With the little strength that he had left he beckoned Nejla to him. She leant across the bed with her ear close to his lips. He whispered quietly yet distinctly. She sat back looking uneasy, then turned and looked at the other end of the room. How tragic, she thought to herself, that these hospital rooms are so drab, people need brightness when they are ill. She was jolted as Hamid asked her urgently, 'What did he say?'

'Oh Hamid,' she glanced at his father, 'it's hard to tell you.'

'Nejla,' Hamid raised his voice. 'Tell me what he said.'

Nejla reached out and took her father-in-law's hand and held it firmly, then looked at Hamid. 'He said he had a dream last night of a man dressed in a shining white robe coming to him with a message.'

She looked down at the ground and hesitated, then looked up at Hamid nervously. Hamid said impatiently, 'Go on, what else did he say?'

Nejla regained her composure and spoke with confidence. 'He said the man in his dream told him that I could tell him the message from God's word that would fill the emptiness of his soul for all eternity.'

Hamid stood up and stared in disbelief. 'Nejla, I don't believe this, you're just . . .'

Hamid was interrupted by his father gasping and reaching out his hand. '. . . the truth, Hamid . . .' his father spluttered. Hamid stood silently looking first at Nejla and then his father, and then walked out of the room.

Nejla pulled the chair closer to the bed and held her father-in-law's hand in her own. There was a tree outside the window with a little bird singing; the sun came shimmering into the room, making even this drab place dance with brightness. Nejla leaned forward and spoke softly. 'You are going to die soon, you know this, don't you?'

Hamid's father gave a slight movement of his head.

'After you die you will go to God's judgement seat and give an account of your life.' Tears began to well up in Nejla's eyes, yet she remained composed. 'Your life has been good, you have been honest, you have helped many people, but you know that something is still missing inside your heart. You know, and God knows, there is sin in your heart you cannot take away.'

Again Hamid's father nodded slightly in agreement. 'God has a wonderful garden. In His garden only beauty is allowed. There is no sadness or imperfection there. Mankind has sinned and so because God loves us, He has provided a way for us to be made clean so that we can live in His garden with Him. If we don't want to be made clean, then we must be separated from God for all eternity.'

'But how can we be made clean?' gasped out Hamid's father.

'The Bible tells us that Jesus lived a perfect life, and then He died on the cross to pay the penalty for our sins. Three days later, He rose up from the grave, proving that God had found His sacrifice for sin to be acceptable. If you believe this, then God will cleanse your heart from all sin and make you perfect in His sight. Then when you die, you will go to live in God's garden, which is heaven.'

Nejla looked pleadingly at the old man who was now in the last moments of his earthly life. For a moment she felt a surge of guilt at being so bold, yet he had asked her for the message.

Hamid came back into the room and walked across to the window. Why had all this happened in his life; everything seemed so complex; life, death, marriage, loyalty? He raised both hands and covered his face. 'Oh God', he thought, 'if only life was not so painful!'

Nejla continued to sit close to the bed. 'Do you understand?' she whispered softly. Hamid's father nodded. Then something strange and almost sacred happened before their eyes.

The old man's face was suddenly filled with a smile; the deep agonising expression of pain that had been on his face had vanished. There was an unexplainable sense of peace and purity in the room. Slowly he moved his hand upward as if reaching out, and the expression on his face was like that of a little child receiving a present.

Hamid stood rooted to the spot. Nejla looked on in awe, tears streaming down her face.

That old and contorted face was now beaming with an expression of great joy.

'Music! I can hear music, it's lovely.' For one moment Hamid's father began to sit up as if welcoming his dearest friend. The sun poured through the window and shone full into his face, intensifying even more the beauty of the moment.

Then he slumped back upon his bed, his eyes closed, yet still with an expression of peace upon his face. There was an aura of contentment surrounding his lifeless body. He was now in the presence of God, no longer bound by a weak body and the disappointments of life. Instead, he was being embraced by a God who cares and is love itself; not alone at the judgement seat of God, but alive in God's garden and able to enjoy the warmth of His presence forever.

The room was still, with just the sound of the two young people's breathing, which in the quietness of this holy moment seemed unusually loud to them both. Hamid leaned forward to his father's lifeless body. 'Papa, Papa!' He buried his head in the bedclothes and wept loudly, 'Papa, Papa.'

Nejla, with tears streaming down her face, reached across and put her arms around her tired, burdened husband. 'Hamid, I'm sorry that your father is gone, but he is happy now. He is in God's garden; his soul is at peace at last.'

# 11

# Death all around

A large crowd stood around the coffin. The women were standing to one side, and many of them were weeping and wailing loudly. A number of the men were also weeping. Hamid's father had been a popular man and had been respected throughout the community.

Hamid's mother stood alone, holding a handful of earth, with little bits trickling through her fingers. She walked up to the coffin and dropped the earth inside. Slowly, each of the guests, went through the same ritual. As Nejla moved forward, Hamid's mother turned towards her with a bitter scowl. It was obvious to everyone that there was a deep hatred in her heart for her son's young bride. She cried out in a wailing scream, pointing her finger at Nejla. 'You, you, you have polluted his soul, you evil, evil witch!'

Nejla stood rooted to the ground, bewildered by what was happening. Feeling the cold sensation of evil streaming towards her, she silently prayed that

God would protect her. As the stream of verbal abuse intensified, Hamid quickly grabbed Nejla's arm and hurried her away from the graveyard.

Hussein tried to calm his mother, but as Hamid and Nejla turned the corner leading to the main road, they could still hear her cursings going on and on.

'I don't know how you stood it, Nejla.'

Leila was holding her sister's hand as they sat together in the living-room.

'Well, it was terrible, but it was hard for her losing her husband.'

'Oh God! I can't stand the thought that I've got to live there in a few months' time when I marry Hussein.'

Nejla looked around the room and remembered those days when they had both been children, and the many happy times they had spent together. There was the big table that they had both hidden under to play shops or hospitals. Life had changed. They were both beginning to experience the harsh realities of adult life, which had been unknown or distant to them before, almost every day.

Nejla had also seen how her mother had begun to feel the pressures of both her daughters entering married life. They had been her companions when her husband had been so rough with her, sometimes even beating her. Now the thought of living alone just with him was filling her with despair.

'Nejla,' said Leila, 'you know when we were walking through the woods that time and I prayed? Well, it's been coming to my mind a lot these days. I wonder if our engagement is going to break up.'

She looked across to her sister. 'If it does, I really do think I will become a believer like you.'

'Oh Leila, be careful, you mustn't play games with God. We can't bargain with Him.' She reached out and gently touched Leila's face. 'Leila, Hamid's father became a believer just minutes before he died. His death wasn't horrible, it was actually beautiful to see his face turn so peaceful. But if he hadn't decided the moment he did, it could have been too late. I don't want it to be too late for you.'

'Well, I'm not thinking of dying yet!'

At that moment their mother came weeping into the room. 'Aysha is dead!' she sobbed. Both girls were horrified, for Aysha was only a little older than Leila. She had been married when she was fourteen to a brutal man twice her age, who drank heavily. 'Her husband killed her.'

'Oh God, Mama, what happened? She was pregnant. The grizzly brute! The filthy dirty pig! Oh God, what is this world we are in?' Leila cried out in anger.

'Mama, what happened?' Nejla put her arms around her mother and gently led her over to the couch.

Her mother looked pale and yet angry. Her face expressed her feelings of helplessness at being unable to do anything to change the situation.

'He said that she was using the excuse of having morning sickness so that she wouldn't have to get his breakfast ready on time. He said she was just lazy. Then he kicked her in the stomach and walked out of the house. She haemorrhaged and died. The police have got him, and Abdulla said they really beat him up badly.'

'Beat him?' Leila screamed, thrusting her arms in the air. 'They should torture him, make him suffer, let me do it! I would take a knife and stick . . .'

'Leila, stop it!' Nejla stood up and held her sister's shoulders firmly in her hands. 'That sweet girl cannot be helped by revenge.'

'Revenge? Yes, I want revenge. It's okay for you, Nejla. You are a lady priest or something. But that could be you or me out there dead on the ground. Men are pigs, they are all pigs!'

Nejla looked deeply into her sister's eyes and then across to her mother. 'They are not all pigs and we can love them with God's help, even when it seems impossible.'


'You know, for a small town this place seems riddled with trouble.' Hussein glanced across at Hamid. The room was dark and an atmosphere of mourning pervaded it. Although everyone had been upset at the death of their father, it had not been unexpected, because of his long illness. In contrast, the tragic killing of Aysha had been sudden and the whole community had been shocked.

Some old women talked of curses being put on the town by a stranger who had travelled through recently. Others, feeling confused, had no answers. Yet the community was stunned with the loss of two people who had been well liked.

'I told you, Hamid, it's hopeless. The best thing that you and I could do would be to join the Merchant Navy.'

'It's crazy, this whole town is crazy.'

'Have you heard the latest? Mama is saying that your wife changed Papa's religion just before he died.'

Hamid looked away nervously. Nejla, the one who filled his heart with love, whom everyone felt was so sweet, was now the focal point for a new scandal; a scandal much worse than the one that surrounded Hussein's divorce.

'Let's face it, Hamid, you've got to live for yourself. Treat the women as animals that give you pleasure, and step on anyone who gets in your way.' Hussein lit another cigarette and picked up his newspaper. The room was depressing and Hamid felt as if it were closing in on him. What would happen next to shake his life?

# 12

# *Lake of tears*

'What did you really tell my father before he died?'
The trees seemed so fresh and green, yet the
expression on Hamid's face was tortured.

'What did you tell your mother I said?' Nejla's face
was peaceful but the strain of the last few weeks had
begun to show.

'I wouldn't have said anything if I had realised it
was going to cause trouble. I just told her that he had
a dream and that you showed him what it meant.'

A squirrel darted up the side of Young Love,
making them both smile and momentarily lifting the
heaviness that weighed down on them.

'I just told him about God having a special sacrifice
for sin and that if we believed in this and asked His
forgiveness, He would take the sin away.'

'I'm confused, Nejla. I feel torn between all that
my mother wants from me and the part of me that
loves you. When I'm with you I feel that just being
together is all that's important; yet when I'm with

Mama, she makes me feel confused about the two of us, as if it's wrong for me to love you.'

'Oh darling Hamid, I want you to love your mother, I really do. I'm just so sorry that she feels this way about me. I've tried to talk to her but she just pushes me away. It's really hard to know what to do.'

Hamid turned and looked at their tree. 'I wonder if the twist in Young Love's trunk is a sign that our lives, which started so beautifully together, will end up twisted or broken.'

'Hamid, darling, please don't talk like that. I love you.'

Nejla had got up early and, having completed all her household duties, decided to visit her sister. As she was going through the door, the thought came into her mind, 'Take your Bible'. Turning back, she picked up the Bible, carefully wrapped it, placed it in her bag and then left the house.

Several days earlier, her mother-in-law had decided that at the first chance she had, she would go into Nejla and Hamid's room. She longed to find something special that belonged to Nejla, destroy it and then leave a curse in its place. Hearing the outer door close, she hurried to the window and saw Nejla walking down the path.

Feeling a mounting excitement, she moved across to the cupboard where she had hidden the curse that she had paid a woman to write. Then, with determination, she mounted the stairs to Nejla and Hamid's room. Closing the door behind her, she surveyed the room. Then, deliberately, she began opening doors and cupboards, throwing all the contents carelessly onto the floor. After a while she found a little notebook that contained some poems Nejla had written. With a cold, calculated desire to hurt her son's wife, she got a dish and tore the little book to shreds. Then, laying the curse on top of it, she laughed. The cruel, cackling sound cut through the silence of the house as she imagined the terror that would strike Nejla's heart when she found the curse.

That morning as Nejla had been reading her Bible, a verse seemed to leap out of the pages; 'All things work together for good to those who love God.' Now as she returned home from visiting her family these words ran through her mind. Surely *all* things included good things and bad things! 'Oh Lord,' she prayed, deeply moved. 'Thank You for this promise that You will work everything out for good. Lord, I trust You – even for the hard things that may happen to me in the future.'

As she walked up the stairs a thought came into her mind. 'You don't really trust the Lord, you just think you do.'

Standing outside the door she bowed her head. 'Lord, You promised – *all* things.' Then turning the knob she entered, halting in horror on the doorstep. The room, which had been left so tidy, was in a shambles. Slowly a tear trickled down her cheek. Could her mother-in-law have done this? 'Oh Lord, help me!'

Then, painfully, she began picking things up and reorganising the room. After about half an hour her eyes fell on the dish with its shredded paper. Picking up the curse, she looked up. 'Thank You, Lord, that I don't have to fear any curse. Nothing can harm me that's outside Your perfect will.' Then deliberately she tore up the curse and threw it out of the window, where the wind immediately blew it away.

Smiling, she looked down again. 'Oh no!' The cry was wrenched from her and tears began to flow at her dawning comprehension of the loss of her poems, which she had written so lovingly. 'Why, Lord, why?'

Quietly a thought entered her mind. 'But I protected the Bible for you, didn't I?'

The Bible! Running to her bag, she tenderly lifted the Bible out and holding it nestled in her arms, she began to thank God for His wonderful care, for she knew with certainty that if the Bible had been in the room, it would have been destroyed as well.

'Mama, why do you hate Nejla so much?' Hamid stood looking pleadingly at his mother. Her face had taken on a more vindictive look since her husband's death. Her eyes revealed a deep bitterness and even her presence in the room seemed to generate an atmosphere of tension and animosity.

'When you were just a baby, Habbibba came to visit me,' she said. Habbibba was Hamid's father's sister, who was much older than his father, but had never been married. She had spent most of her time going from house to house with the older women and reading the women's fortunes from their coffee cups. Hamid just vaguely remembered her as she had died when he was still a small child.

'She told me that you and I had a special

relationship. If you loved anyone else more than me at my death, then we would be separated by a huge lake of tears after the day of judgement. Now Nejla has taken you away from me. She pretends to be kind and sweet on the outside, but inside she is a snake who has a gentle voice but a poisonous bite. She turned your father's heart away from the faith by casting a spell on him. When they washed his body before going to the graveyard, people said he had a strange look on his face, quite different from anything they had ever seen before.'

Hamid's mother drew closer to him and looked deeply into his eyes. 'Divorce her, Hamid, divorce her and I will arrange another wedding for you. There's a beautiful young girl about fifteen years old in Abdulla's brother's village. I can get her for you.'

Hamid stepped back as if he had been dealt a physical blow. 'You can't be serious!'

'Serious? I've never been more serious. Do it, Hamid, get rid of her, she is no good. She will only bring trouble to our family.'

Hamid ran from the room and made his way to the woods. Maybe if he could be beside Young Love, perhaps he could find some kind of way through the confusion that surrounded him. He could see in his mind the look of peace on his father's face when he had sat up suddenly, listening to some kind of heavenly music. Hamid felt absolute wonder at the dream his father had had.

He could hear Nejla's tender voice clearly in his mind speaking of the garden, of sin, and the sacrifice that gets us back into the garden. He could see Hussein spit into the fire with utter contempt for love, and yet he sensed a wholesomeness about his wife's love that he had never known before.

He stood alone in front of the tree they had both begun to love so much. Suddenly he dropped to his knees and began to weep in anguish. He loved Nejla, and yet he felt pulled towards his mother. He wanted to stay married but he felt he couldn't face much more pressure. Shaking his head from side to side, weeping, Hamid prayed, 'God, change this situation, so I can please my mother and still keep my wife.'

'Why didn't you come to the funeral?' Leila had a deeply mournful look on her face as she talked to Nejla. They walked down towards the river. The grass was long and glistened with drops of water from the rain that had fallen the night before.

'Leila, I was with Aysha the day before she was killed. She sent for me because she needed help. She was lonely and frightened of her husband.'

'Did you tell her about God's garden?'

'Yes, and because I had been seen going into her house, I felt it best to stay away, because of all the trouble lately.'

'Oh Nejla, it was terrible.' They stood beside the river and looked at the stream that was beginning to swell from the rains. They both thought back to when it had been just a trickle, the day before Nejla's wedding.

'I've never seen anything like it. Aysha's older brother was going wild, he really loved her. He completely collapsed by the grave in tears. Then, springing to his feet, he suddenly started screaming and saying that he was going to kill her husband! When they started to put the earth on the coffin, he cut his hand and rubbed it in the earth, vowing that if he hadn't killed her husband by the end of the month, he would kill himself.

'Nej, has this town always been like this? It's just terrible, all this bitterness and pain.'

# 13

# The stranger

Hussein, at times like this, needed to be away from everyone. An inner tension seemed to build up within him that could find no release. Being near people just made things worse.

As he walked up the narrow winding path leading into the hills, he felt relief at being away from Hamid and his mother. Now that his father was gone, his life seemed futile and meaningless.

From the top of the hill he could look right across the valley. The winding river seemed so still and harmless from up here, yet he knew from bitter experience how dangerous it could be. As a little boy he had fallen in once. Fortunately one of the men from the town, passing by, had jumped in and dragged him out. No sooner had he been out of the water, still coughing and spluttering from the water, than his rescuer had hit him several times around the head for going so near the river.

He could also see his own home clearly from here.

There was a thin wisp of smoke coming from the chimney, which seemed to drift upwards like a piece of string dangling from the sky. At the far end of the town was the mosque with its minaret pointing up to heaven. He could remember as a child the fund-raising activities that had preceded the building of that minaret. His father had told him that it was an important thing for their small town to have completed such a building. In the village in the mountains where his father had grown up, the mosque was only a tiny one-roomed building.

The mountains seemed so distant to Hussein, but he sometimes wished he had grown up there. Life was less complicated there. If his wife had been found to be unfaithful in a village like that, then either her father or brother would have killed her without thinking about it. For a moment Hussein sat down on a rock to gaze at his town. Inside himself he felt again the great welling up of tension, which seemed to have no way out. How alone and isolated he felt!

*'Selam Aleikem!'* The words seemed to come from nowhere. He looked up into the face of an elderly man, perhaps in his seventies. *'Aleikem Selam!'* Hussein replied. The stranger had a friendly look on his face. Deep lines, etched into his face, looked as if they had been drawn with Indian ink. He wore a well-shaped, almost snow-white beard. In this area, a man of his age would only have a beard if he had been to Mecca.

'How are you? You look troubled,' said the old man, looking genuinely concerned.

Hussein smiled and said, 'Nothing is wrong. Where have you come from, Uncle?'

The old man looked towards the mountains and raised his hand slightly as if he was going to point.

'Oh, a long way on the other side of the mountain. You say nothing is wrong, but your eyes tell me that you are sad, confused; even angry.'

Hussein was completely taken aback by such frankness from a total stranger. Somehow this old man seemed harmless; even the way he looked at him was disarming, but his eyes seemed to see right into him.

'Tell me, Uncle,' Hussein said, looking away, 'is life so hard, so disappointing, and so painful for everyone?'

'Look at me.' The old man smiled. Hussein turned and looked into his gentle face.

'Life is hard for everyone, yet for some life is harder than for others. For you, your life seems hard; harder and more disappointing than others you know. Yet your life is easy compared to a man in my home village who lost his house, his animals, his children, and his wife in the big earthquake. Yet even he is probably better off than someone somewhere else.

'Look at the river,' he pointed down the valley. Hussein felt compelled to look. 'See how the river twists and turns? From up here we can see all the places the river goes to, we can see round the corners that you cannot see down in the town. Life is like that river. Sometimes it goes over rocks, sometimes it turns corners, and like the river we cannot see things from down where we are; we do know that the river has a beginning and an end; so life has its beginning and end, with corners and rocks, but only God sees all our life as we see this river from up here.'

Hussein had never heard such words, and in a strange way they seemed to relieve his tension.

Hussein took a cigarette from his pocket and lit it slowly, looking intently down at the river for several moments. He turned to face his new-found friend, but the old man had gone. Suddenly, Hussein felt a flush of fear run through him.

He jumped up and ran down the hill. Turning the corner, he just saw the old man climb a large rock to another path a long way below. He opened his mouth to call out, but hesitated. The old man had obviously wanted to share those words with him and then leave. Slowly he walked back to his original place, overlooking the river. How odd to receive such wisdom from such a strange source just when he needed encouragement!

'Only God sees all our lives.' The words seemed to burn within him. 'Only God sees all our lives'! For a moment Hussein felt that the *kismet* fate of his fathers was different from what this old man had shared with him, but what was that difference?


Hussein and Hamid walked along the main road, where no traffic was to be seen.

'I can't tell you how confused I feel about all this.' Hussein spoke nervously as if his confidence and attitudes towards life itself were threatened.

'What do you mean? I thought you were the one who had it all worked out. Remember, "live for pleasure"?'

Hussein stopped and looked across to the

mountains. Now, they were a greenish brown blending into an almost copper sky.

'Did you know the police beat Aysha's husband badly? Well, now he's blind. The official story is that he fell down the stairs with handcuffs on, but actually the police beat him too much and that's why he's gone blind. The thing that has unnerved me is that it could have been me. You know, Hamid, I think I'm really rotten. I know I'm rotten to women anyway. I really want to change.'

Hamid stopped and looked back towards the town, disconcerted. A man with a horse and cart was making his way slowly up the road. Was anything to be relied on in this world? His confusion had grown with his father's peaceful death, his mother's hatred for his wife, Aysha's death, and his brother Hussein, who had been so hard, and yet was now wanting to become good. His brother's earlier words had been right; 'This town *is* crazy!' he thought to himself.

# 14

# Cut down

The burly woodman stood in the doorway as Hamid's mother reached into a tin box in the corner of the cupboard. Taking out some money, she returned to the man.

'Here, this will cover the costs. It's the tree with the twist in it. Cut it down and then chop it up into bits.'

It had taken Hamid's mother some time to realise the importance of Young Love to the young couple. Now Young Love would be cut down and each swing of the woodman's axe would be like a blow to Nejla's soul.

'Nejla!' Even as that name came into her thoughts, she spat on the ground.

Nejla sat down on her old bed. It was good to be back in her parents' house again. She looked around the room and could see where the bottle of tablets and cup lay by the table. The little teddy bear was tucked into Leila's bed with his head lying on the pillow, giving a lifelike effect.

'Nej, it's incredible! Read this.' Jumping up, Leila handed her a letter, and then started pacing up and down the room.

'Sit down, you're making me nervous,' Nejla smiled.

'Just read it!'

'Dear Leila,' (read Nejla)

'This is the hardest thing I have ever done in my life and I am not sure if even doing it is right or not.

'The things that have happened round here recently have made me think very deeply about my life and my future.

'I have done many bad things of which I am not proud. My attitude to our getting married was quite calculated. I had decided to marry to have sons, to have someone to wait on me, and to live for my own pleasure. I know that people talk about me and say that I am a bad person. In many ways they are right.

'What I am trying to say is that even though you may hear stories about me, and many of them are true, I want to change. I just need help, because I don't know how to change on my own.

'I hope this letter makes sense.

'Hussein'

'Do you think it's really from him or is it one of his

friends playing a joke?' Leila held her breath, not quite sure what she wanted to hear.

'No, it's his handwriting, I've seen it before.'

Leila sighed. 'He really sounds sincere, but do you think I can trust him?'

Nejla stood up, walked across to the window, then turned to Leila. 'I think God is working in both your lives to prepare you for the time when you really give your lives to Him.'

Nejla carried on talking, turning back towards the window. 'God cares about . . .' Down at the clump of trees in the distance she could see the woodcutter swinging his axe. 'Young Love!' The cry seemed wrenched from the depths of her being. 'He is cutting my tree down!'

She rushed out of the room, down the stairs, and through the garden that led to the open fields where the clump of trees was.

As she arrived the woodman was leaving. Young Love was completely cut down. The woodman hadn't understood why the tree was to be cut down, but he didn't really care as long as he got the right money for the job. As he walked home, he wondered if the old lady had thought that the tree was cursed. He had been called in on other occasions to cut down trees that were thought to have a curse on them.

Nejla knelt by the stump of her tree and wept. The tree was just a tree to the rest of the world, but for her and Hamid Young Love was special. Leaning forward, she laid her head on the stump and began to cry, praying, 'Oh Lord, who would do such a thing? Who?' After a short while, she prayed brokenly, 'Lord, I forgive them, help me forgive them.'

Later that day, Hamid returned home and stood for a moment in the doorway, looking at his young wife. Nejla turned when she realised he was there and, as was her custom, immediately stopped her work and came over to welcome him home. Tonight, though, he immediately sensed that something was wrong.

'Are you okay? You look unhappy. Has Mother been getting at you again?'

Nejla shook her head to tell him it wasn't that and then burst into tears.

'Hey, what's wrong? Tell me.'

Nejla looked up; her lips were trembling as she tried to regain control over herself.

'Someone has cut Young Love down,' she whispered, and then fell into her husband's arms and wept.

'Nejla, don't cry. We can find another special tree,' he reassured her gently. Inwardly, however, Hamid felt as if something important to his own happiness had come to an end.

# 15

# Serap

'Come in, come in!' Leila tried to look pleased to see Serap, Hussein's first wife, who was standing at the door.

Serap looked defeated; her face was pale and her hair, which always used to have so much shine in it, seemed lifeless and flat.

'Come on, sit down. It's lovely to see you. How are you, Serap?' Leila tried not to feel threatened by Hussein's ex-wife and then realised she was comparing herself with her visitor.

'Leila, is it really true? Are you going to marry Hussein?'

Leila felt a conflict rising inside her. Should she tell Serap that Hussein had said he wanted to change? Wouldn't that mean that Serap's family would try and bring about a reconciliation?

'Yes, it is true. Do you hate me because of it?'

'Oh Leila, of course not.' Serap sat a little uneasily on the chair and looked nervously around the room.

'Actually, there is a reason for my coming here.'

Serap began hesitantly to share her unhappy story with the younger girl. 'Oh Leila, it was horrible! Before the wedding, Mrs Rifat took me on my own into a room and began to threaten me. She said that from now on I would have to obey her, and that it was no longer my own mother or even Hussein who was important. I would have to submit to her alone. She said lots of other things and I was frightened. I was confused, and so I didn't say anything to anyone. After the wedding we went back to Hussein's house. His mother took me to her room and Hussein went out. Then she started swearing at me, and hit me, saying that I had had another man and that I was cheap and dirty. Leila, I don't know anything about men. I had been playing with dolls and helping with the housework in my father's house until my wedding day.'

Leila reached out to Serap's face and touched it gently. 'I believe you, Serap.'

'Well, she made me sleep on the floor in her room that night. I was so scared, thinking she was going to kill me. The next morning, she went off with Hussein. When he finally came back, he was furious. He beat me, shouting all the time, "I trusted you!", and then he just ran out. I didn't see him for days and days and was kept a virtual prisoner in his mother's room. Then one day when she was out, I managed to slip out and run home. My family were really annoyed. For weeks on end I was pushed around and taken to see a doctor who did some tests. It was horrible; the doctor said I was still a virgin but my parents didn't believe him, and everyone turned against me. In the end the marriage was annulled, because we had never lived together as man and wife.

'Leila, the reason I'm telling you all this is that Hussein turned really bitter after that. I think he's very confused. It's almost as if his mother has some strange control over her sons.'

'Oh Serap,' Leila's heart was breaking as she thought of the hurt and humiliation this young woman had been through, 'I'm so sorry you had to go through all this, but what's going to happen to you now?'

Serap shrugged her shoulders, and pressed both her lips together, as if to say, only God knows.

Leila reached over and pressed her hand again. 'Serap, even though things may be difficult, I want you to know I will always be your friend.'

The rain seemed to be washing away the tension inside the house as well as the dirt outside, as it streamed down around the house. The sun, bursting through the dark clouds, seemed to be a promise of a fresh start.

'I think it's good that my mother has gone away for the weekend.'

Nejla's eyes sparkled at the thought of Hamid and herself being truly alone. 'I hope she has a good time at your aunt's house.'

Nejla snuggled up to Hamid as they looked out of the window across the open fields. 'I'm glad we can be alone. It has been so tense recently with all the trouble,' he said.

Hamid looked deep into Nejla's dark eyes,

something he always enjoyed doing for he could feel the acceptance and warmth radiating from her. Somehow, too, his problems seemed to lose some of their sting.

However, the confusion of the past few months had left him feeling empty and tired inside. He longed for his mother to accept his young wife, but as the days went by, the intensity of her hatred only grew stronger.

'How do you feel about your tree?' Hamid asked, walking over to the table and pouring some fresh mint tea into a glass.

Nejla turned and smiled. Behind the smile, her eyes betrayed her feelings of pain. 'Well, it's hard, because it was so special for us. I just can't understand why your mother would do such a thing.'

Hamid sipped his tea, then walked over to the window again. 'Nej, it's hard to explain this but I feel kind of pulled between you and my mother.'

Nejla had heard this before, but the look of interest in her eyes made Hamid feel it was the first time he was sharing it with her.

'When I was little, I suppose about six or seven years old, I fell off the wall behind our house. Hussein came and fetched me when he heard me crying. When he'd taken me into the house, my mother came, took me by the hand, and led me over to that big table that's in the front room.'

Nejla held out her hand to Hamid, inviting him to sit down beside her.

'Well, she picked me up, and put me on the table. Sternly, she told me that I had fallen off the wall as a punishment because I didn't love her with all my heart. Ever since, I've been afraid that I might not love her enough.'

'Oh Hamid, that was hard for you, but love shouldn't grow out of fear.' She reached out and touched his cheek gently, stroking his face. 'I'm sure your mother didn't mean to frighten you but, Hamid darling, loyalty based on fear isn't real love.' Nejla paused as if searching for the right words. 'When we grow up afraid of God, afraid that if we make a wrong move He will hit us, we're not seeing God as He really is.

'He wants us to love and obey Him, not out of fear or just because He tells us to, but because we feel safe with Him and can trust Him with our lives.'

Hamid reached across to Nejla and kissed her. It was still raining, but a stillness filled the room with a warm sense of security that Hamid could not explain.

'Nejla,' Hamid's eyes began to fill with tears and his lower lip quivered, 'I love you, but I'm afraid that if I don't love my mother and do what she says, something terrible will happen. It's like falling off the wall all over again.'

Hamid began to cry. Nejla quickly reached out and put her arms around him. 'Nejla, Nejla, I'm so afraid, so afraid.'

'Hamid, dear Hamid, we can make it with God's help, we really can. God can take away all your fear and confusion, and give you a whole new life.'


'Come in, Leila!' Nejla kissed her sister on each

cheek, and then hugged her. 'Hamid is at work, Hussein is out, and my mother-in-law is away, so we can have a lovely chat.'

Leila's life had begun to change recently. Serap's visit, as well as the letter from Hussein, had made her think. Looking back, her prayer that God would break up her proposed marriage now seemed wrong. It disturbed her that she had taken spiritual things so lightly.

As the two sisters sat and drank tea together, Leila began to talk about her inner conflicts. 'Nej, I don't know if being good and helping people is enough. I feel like there's something missing inside me. I can't explain it, but something inside is terribly insecure and dissatisfied.'

Nejla reached out for her Bible and slowly flicked through the pages. Leila moved closer so that she could see the book as well.

'Look at what God's word says, Leila. "I am come that they might have life and have it more abundantly." This is Jesus speaking. If people's lives were really complete and perfect, Jesus would never have needed to come into the world.'

'Oh Nej, I know that Jesus said wonderful things, but it's not for me.' Standing up, Leila walked across Nejla's little room. 'I've been thinking that if I do marry Hussein, I just don't want to get into a heavy conflict over religion with him or his mother. God only knows how tough it has been for you!'

Nejla listened patiently and lovingly as Leila poured out her fears and frustrations.

'Besides, it would be so hard when the children came, with things like circumcision.'

'Leila, belief in God doesn't affect things like that. God wants to change our hearts. He doesn't tell us to change our culture, in fact He doesn't even say we are to change our religion. What Jesus says in the Bible is this; if you have a heavy burden or you are labouring and striving, come to Him in faith and He will give you rest and peace of mind.'

The two girls bent again over the pages of the Bible, and the precious moments they had together sped away.

A cluster of violets brought by Nejla was all that relieved the barrenness of Aysha's grave. It was some distance from the general area, and even this seclusion reminded Hussein of the irony that through no fault of her own, this sweet girl's isolation in life still held her in death.

Although Hussein had never particularly liked graveyards, he somehow felt compelled to come and stand by this grave, a reminder to him of how someone so innocent and well-loved had been hated and finally destroyed. Hussein, like Leila, had been going through a process in his thinking. He thought of the suddenness of death, the finality of it all, the fanfare of birth and circumcision, the hope and dreams that seemed to culminate in the anti-climax and the disappointment of death. He wondered where Aysha's spirit was now. One of the old ladies in the village had said it would haunt her husband until he died a slow and miserable death.

And yet he couldn't imagine Aysha doing such a thing. He thought of heaven and of hell. Here in the graveyard they seemed so real. Yet who knew the answers? The religious people only seemed to have superficial answers; he felt they lacked any real, deep understanding of the issues that affected him. As he stood and thought about these things, Nejla kept coming into his mind. 'Perhaps she has the answer,' he thought, '. . . perhaps she knows where Aysha's spirit is.'

'Oh my God, it never ends around here!' Leila looked pale and wan as she stumbled in through the doorway.

'What on earth has happened?' Leila's mother asked, almost afraid to find out after what had happened in the last year.

'Aysha's husband is dead.'

'What? How did it happen? Was it Aysha's brother?'

'First Aysha, and now this! Surely this revenge killing can't go on and on.'

'Quick, tell me what happened!'

'He was being taken from the prison to the court when Aysha's brother jumped out from nowhere and shot him dead. Before the police could do anything, he turned the gun on himself and fired. He's dead too. His last words were "God is great". Oh Mama, how can God be great when He does nothing to stop all this insane hatred and killing?'

Mother and daughter looked at each other, speechless and afraid.

# 16

# *The curse*

Nejla felt the need to spend time reading her Bible, and so she hurried through her duties. The mirror she was polishing reflected a girl with the poise and confidence of someone who was loved. Nejla was secure in the love of her God, and her assurance gave her an aura of peace and tranquillity.

The experiences she had been passing through had caused a deepening of character, which was reflected in her face. The lines of sorrow only seemed to increase her beauty, as the sorrow had brought her a new depth of gentleness and compassion. At the moment, though, her face was slightly drawn, and an anxious frown wrinkled her brow.

As she sat down, she looked around her, mentally checking that all her duties had been done, and then opened her Bible. After reading for a time, she paused to think over what she had read, and a sense of wonder filled her heart. Kneeling down by the side of the bed, she began to pour out her heart to God in prayer. For some time she could only tell God of her grief and confusion. Then, still weeping, she prayed; 'Lord, I love You. I don't understand why these things are happening, but I trust You. Thank You for Your promise to be with me always. Thank You for this situation.' She looked around the little room that was their home, at the little bookcase that Hamid had made and the cabinet with all her plants neatly arranged. She continued to thank God for His presence, for her home, her husband, and for her problems, even thanking Him for her mother-in-law.

As she prayed, she sensed great waves of love passing over her and through her. She was reassured that she belonged to God and that nothing could happen to her from which He could not bring something good. She felt refreshed. She sensed that the burdens she had been carrying for the last few weeks were being lifted off her shoulders one by one. It was a wonderful experience, as she let go of all the things that so weighed her down and was able to feel God's love and care for her in a new way.

She found herself weeping tears of joy and the more she wept, the more this awareness of relief and release filled her soul. Nejla turned her face towards heaven; a ray of sunlight glanced through the window and fell full onto her face. She thought back to the time when she had imagined she was looking at the throne of God and her heart was full of peace. With compassion, she began to pray that her mother-in-law would come to understand that she too was loved by God.

Several weeks had passed and now Hamid paced up and down the room nervously, as his mother lay motionless on her bed. 'You look okay, Mama. I'm sure you will be better tomorrow.' Hamid knew that he was lying to his mother and to himself. He was worried. She looked so ill; a shadow of her former self.

'Let me get Nejla to come in and look after you,' he urged.

'No! I don't want her near me. If you really want to help me and please me, you can divorce her.'

'Mama, surely you can't want me to divorce her now! You know she is carrying my child.'

'Any child that woman bears will have a curse on it! You are my son and you must obey me.'

'Oh Mama, if you told me to die, I would do it without question, but how can you ask me to do a thing like this? It's not right.'

Hamid's mother turned onto her side and stared blankly beyond her son's shoulder. 'If I die . . .'

'Oh, stop it! You aren't going to die.'

'. . . if I die, and you love Nejla more than me, the two of us will be separated forever by the lake of tears. Forever, Hamid.'

Reaching over to the glass of water on the table, then lifting his mother, Hamid helped her to drink. He felt himself entangled in a web from which there was no escape, and slowly that web seemed to be closing in on him.

As his mother drifted into sleep, he wondered if he could really divorce Nejla. He thought of the love they had shared so intensely, if only for such a short time. He thought of the happy times around their

tree, Young Love. He imagined the joy of becoming a
father. Then he thought about his mother's words
and the way she had had Young Love cut down, and
he felt his world had begun to crumble around him.

'Nej, I can't even tell you how I feel.' Leila had just
shared with her sister the story that Serap had told
her. Now, the thought of marrying Hussein seemed
almost bearable.

'Come, sit over here.' Nejla moved a chair into
position for Leila, who seemed suddenly so full of
life.

'Actually Nej, I've worked it out about God.'

'What do you mean?'

'Well, I think different people need different
experiences. For you, it has to be deep and spiritual.
For me, well, I just want to be good and help people
in trouble.'

Nejla stood up and walked across to a plant
hanging from a little wicker basket. 'Leila, don't
misunderstand me when I say this, but being good, as
you call it, isn't enough.'

Leila joined her sister, slipping her arm into
Nejla's. 'I think what I want is to be like you; loving,
kind, and gentle; but I just don't want to become
religious.'

Nejla smiled at her sister. God would answer her
prayers for Leila, she thought, in His own time.

# 17

# *Serap's release*

Serap had lost the desire to live. She moved around in a trance, responding mechanically to the demands of everyday life. Her hair, which once had been bouncy and shiny, now lay dull and lifeless. It was as if all the joy of life had been drained from her, leaving only an empty shell.

Most of her time was spent in a small dark room at the top of the house. The curtains were kept drawn and a dark cold atmosphere pervaded the room and seemed to reflect the despair that filled her heart. Occasionally, sounds of children playing somewhere in the street below filtered in through the curtains. No more tears ran down her cheeks. At first, she had wept for many hours by her bedside, without knowing why. Those flooding tears had bathed her soul, leaving a temporary peace. Now there was only a numb pain. Pain surrounded her soul, and some-times made her wish to die; yet she shrank from that desire, afraid of the darkness and finality of death.

She lay on the floor, looking at the ceiling. It occurred to her that she had not washed in three days; indeed, she had hardly left the room. Her older brother had come again the previous evening and spat at her. She no longer wept or pleaded for him to stop his tirade of vicious words. She no longer raised her hands in defence when he struck out at her, beating her in his rage. Fear had begun to grow and welled up in her heart; a deep, unexplained fear. She was afraid of today, of yesterday, and of the future.

'Serap, come here!' Her mother's voice broke through the silence and emptiness of her room. As Serap reached the bottom of the stairs, she noticed Nejla, and her smile, which seemed to radiate warmth and comfort. She tried to stretch out her hand to Nejla to invite her in, but only seemed able to muster enough strength to whisper a word of greeting. Serap's mother bustled by, on her way to the kitchen. For a moment the two just stood and looked at each other. Nejla was fresh, healthy, and alive, while Serap looked pale, almost like a walking corpse, and yet still breathed.

'May I talk with you?' Nejla smiled again, and Serap thought how beautiful she looked.

'Yes, please come in.' Upstairs, Serap sat and looked blankly at her visitor. Nejla reached out, took Serap's hand, squeezed it, then held it firmly as she began to talk. 'Serap, I have been praying for you every day.'

Serap looked at Nejla in wonder. Why would Nejla pray for her? No one cared whether she lived or died.

'Serap, I want you to know that God cares for you and loves you.' Serap felt a well of untapped tears begin to surface. For a moment she was going to let them be released; then she restrained herself and, swallowing, pushed her feelings down inside herself. 'Serap, God accepts you as you are and He understands your pain and even your shame. He does not want to punish you but to bring you forgiveness and freedom from those chains of death that bind you. The Bible says that "God has not given us the spirit of fear, but of power, and of love, and of a sound mind". God wants to give you freedom – even freedom from fear.'

'Freedom, is that possible?' Then, leaning forward with her head in her hands, Serap began to weep. It was as if a dam had burst inside the very depths of her being. As her body shook, the hot tears poured down her face.

Nejla took her in her arms, speaking gently. 'Jesus died to pay the penalty for our sin, Serap. The Bible tells us that the blood of Jesus Christ can cleanse us from *all* sin. We are freed from fear and guilt when we come to Him. Serap, that is what God wants you to experience. If you put your trust in Him, He will cleanse your heart and make your life new.'

'Oh Nejla, can that really happen to me?'

'Yes, of course it can. All you have to do is ask Him. He will not only give you a new heart but He will come to live in your heart, so you need never be alone again. Then whatever problems or heartache you go through, He will share your pain.' Tears filled Nejla's eyes as she saw Serap's tortured soul begin to find release.

'Oh God!' Serap prayed, her eyes still streaming with hot tears, 'I want this freedom that Nejla's Bible

talks about. I do so need You to wash away my sin
and to cleanse me. I believe in You, Jesus, please
come into my life. I've been so afraid, please help
me.'

Nejla reached out to Serap and kissed her on the
cheek. A startling change had come over her. Her
face that had been so empty of expression, though
stained with tears, now radiated a peace and purpose
for living. Life had been reborn within her, for God
Himself had come into Serap's life.

'Nejla, I'm scared about something.' The house
was empty once again with her mother-in-law and
Hussein away, and Hamid at work. Leila looked
disturbed and tired.

'What is it?' Nejla had become Leila's constant
counsellor. The complexities of the two families; the
tragedies, involving so much violence in so short a
time, and her growing faith in God, had caused Nejla
to develop a wisdom far beyond that natural in
someone so young.

'Come, sit down and tell me what's wrong.'

Leila's head was bowed. She closed her hands
slowly and nervously. 'Nej, is Aysha in heaven or
hell?'

'Why do you ask?'

'It's bothering me. This whole religious thing.
What happens to people when they die?'

Nejla touched her sister's arm tenderly. 'Leila, the
Bible says that people, in fact every person in the
world, chooses to be rebellious towards God. That's
what sin is. Not just doing certain kinds of bad

things, but a heart that says that I'm in control of my life, not God. That rebellion leads us, after we have died, to hell, which is a place of horrible isolation and suffering.'

'But surely God wouldn't send people there forever just because they were rebellious?'

Nejla looked at her sister. She was so serious now, so different from a short time ago when she had been so flippant and carefree. Nejla went on, 'We choose by our rebellion to go to hell. God says He wants us to be with Him in heaven, but we reject Him, so in some ways we actually send ourselves to hell. The Bible teaches that God is both holy and righteous. Sin can't enter His presence, but must be judged. Jesus came into the world to take our punishment and to give us a way to escape the result of sin, and God's judgement of that sin.'

'But Nej, what about Aysha?'

Nejla looked around nervously and then drew herself closer to her sister, as if afraid someone might be listening. 'I told you how I went to see Aysha just before she was killed. When I walked through her door, she was smiling. We sat down together and talked. Aysha told me that she had tried to be kind and loving to everyone, even to her husband, who was often unkind to her. She went on to say she felt something was missing in her life; something unexplainable, but real. So I told her about God's garden, things I've told you. By the end of our time together, she was crying. ''This is what I need,'' she kept saying. And then she prayed and asked God to fill her life and take away her sin. It was a wonderful time.'

Nejla smiled and spoke confidently. 'Right now, Leila, Aysha is in heaven. She is there with that precious baby that was in her womb. They are both experiencing the love of God in a way that we can't even begin to imagine. They are at peace, Leila.'

'How can you know for sure?'

'Because God's book says, "Whoever comes to me I will never drive away." '

# 18

# Valley of death

Serap's father walked into the little attic that had been her prison ever since the annulment of her marriage with Hussein.

He looked harshly at her. Since Nejla had visited her, Serap had found freedom and release in knowing Jesus, and her whole life and appearance had changed. Her eyes had regained life. She washed every day and looked after her hair. Her brother still came nearly every evening to beat her and spit in her face. She had come to accept this abuse, and her fear had gone.

She had begun to realise that in a strange, horrible way her brother enjoyed tormenting her. It wasn't anger and shame that drove him on, but rather a twisted and evil heart. Yet now each evening when he came, after he had hit her or spat at her, she would look into his wild eyes and say, 'I forgive you.' Last night when she had said this, he had hardly been able to contain himself for rage. He had picked up a chair

and begun to move towards her, but abruptly had
thrown the chair on the ground and had run out of
the room.

Now as her father stood before her she wondered
what was going to happen. He was a large man who
worked cutting down trees in the forest. He never
attended mosque, and bitterly hated the *hodja* and his
hypocritical religious ways. Her father never came to
her room and she rarely left it, and so this was the
first time she had seen him for weeks.

'You know, daughter, if we were in the mountains,
you would be dead.' He walked across the room and
then turned and faced his daughter. Her face seemed
to be a mixture of pain and suffering somehow
combined with a strange peace and radiance.

'Well, you're lucky because we have got someone
to marry you. There is an Arab man working in the
forests with us; he's staying in another town and
comes down every day. He can hardly speak our
language so he doesn't know anything about what's
going on. You are going to marry him next week and
he will take you back to his country with him. From
that moment, in my eyes, you will be dead; he can do
what he likes with you.'

Serap did not answer, but just stood quietly
looking at her father. He turned and walked out of
the room.

Serap stayed still, stunned as his words penetrated
deep into her soul. His warning, 'He can do what he
likes with you,' seemed to echo in her head. From the
corner of the room she could hear the slow dripping
of water off the roof. Other than that the room was
silent. For one moment she thought she could only

despair. Then a strange thing happened; deep inside her heart she heard a quiet voice, 'Though you walk through the valley of the shadow of death, I am with you.'

She found herself kneeling down and looking upwards as if into heaven. 'Oh God, this is Your voice, I hear You. Thank You that I can know that no matter what happens to me, You are with me.' She remained on her knees. A warm glow seemed to flood through her soul, leaving a deep peace and assurance that she was loved and cared for. She began to weep tears of joy. In the midst of the pain of what tomorrow might hold was a joy that God was her Father and her friend, and would be with her through everything.

# 19

# Into God's garden

'Oh Hamid, come quickly!' Nejla's face showed great concern as she beckoned her husband.

'What's wrong?' asked Hamid.

'It's your mother. She has been taken very ill. I felt for some time that she hasn't been well, but this afternoon she seemed especially weak. I tried to help her but she wouldn't let me near her. In the end, I just had to call the doctor.'

'Where is she now?'

'The doctor arranged for her to go to the hospital. I said I would go with her, but she insisted that I shouldn't go. I didn't know what to do, as she was getting so worked up.'

Hamid looked searchingly at Nejla, expecting to see some kind of relief that his mother had gone, yet all he could see was genuine love and concern. Abruptly Hamid turned and rushed out of the door, without saying another word. Nejla seemed a little surprised that he hadn't said goodbye but put it down to his fear for his mother.

Outside the front entrance of the hospital, he saw Hussein leaning against a tree, smoking a cigarette.

'What are you doing out here smoking? Why aren't you in there with Mama?'

'Take it easy, darling boy.' Hussein stood up, very annoyed by Hamid's reaction. 'She doesn't want me in there. It's you she wants. No one else. She just keeps wailing your name.'

Hamid rushed up the steps to Reception to find out where his mother was.

Her room was silent. In just a few hours his mother had deteriorated rapidly. Her eyes were sunk deep into their sockets. A deathlike pallor seemed to hang over her. 'Mama, it's me.' Hamid reached over and kissed her forehead, feeling shocked by her cold, clammy skin.

'Hamid, my Hamid,' she whined, as her hand slowly stretched out to touch the back of his wrist.

'Mama, I'll do anything for you. Just please don't die, not now, please!' Hamid began to cry. All his life he had lived to please this woman, and now she lay dying. Right now, however, as he sat beside her dying body, he wasn't actually sure if he loved or hated her. Perhaps he felt a mixture of both.

'You love Nejla more than you love me,' she accused him. As she mentioned Nejla, a hard expression came over her face.

'Mama, I'll divorce her if you want. I'll do anything you say but just don't die!'

'Too late, Hamid,' she croaked ominously. 'Too late. You must kill her!'

'Oh, Mama!' The cry rose from the depths of his

body. Surely his mother must be delirious. 'Not that, Mama! I can't do it!'

Her hand, claw-like, reached out and grasped his hand tightly, her fingernails digging into his skin. She spat out the words with venom. 'If you are my son, you will kill Nejla!'

Then, gasping, she exhaled a long rattling groan, and was still; dying in bitterness even as she had lived. Her eyes and her mouth were open, and she looked as sinister in death as her words had been evil in life. Hamid buried his head in the sheets beside her and wept. 'Mama, Mama, don't let me fall off the wall again. I *will* love you, with all my heart.'

Holding the little teddy bear in her hands brought Nejla closer to the past. Leila had brought it to the house earlier; partly as an attempt in her own mind to make a break from her childhood, and prepare for womanhood and her coming marriage to Hussein; and partly from a desire to comfort Nejla.

Looking back, Nejla could see herself as a frightened girl who had now blossomed into womanhood. The last few months had given her a wealth of experience and understanding of people, and had left her with a sense of awe at how quickly the human mind can grow with God's help.

Gently she stroked her stomach. The thought of the coming baby filled her with joy. Perhaps this child would help Hamid to let go of his fears, and to accept his love for his wife as being something good.

The thought of bringing a new life into the world was both exhilarating and a little frightening. It was not the pain of birth that she feared, but rather the responsibility of bringing up a child in a changing world. Television was planned for their town in a year or two; she had heard that, in the bigger cities, people's lives were being affected by what they saw. Most of all she had a feeling of nervousness about bringing something so innocent into the world, to be caught up in the great struggle that she herself was facing; a tangle of superstition and misunderstanding from those who opposed her commitment to God.

The teddy bear that had once lain by her pillow night after night for so many years seemed to represent something distant, but at the same time still comforting to her.

She was sure that Hamid was excited about the baby. He had teased her that it must be a boy and they had laughed together. Tonight would be an evening of hope, despite the sorrow they faced with Hamid's mother being in hospital.

Behind her the door opened slowly. Hamid staggered into the room. His eyes were red and swollen, as if he had been crying. His damp hair lay flat on the side of his face and he looked tired and distraught. His arm hung limply at his side and in his hand was his father's revolver. Nejla heard the door open and turned around, her face joyful. But the warmth of her face changed to a look of anxious questioning.

'Hamid, what's wrong? Why have you got that gun? Why are you looking at me like that? What's happened?' Nejla started to move towards her husband.

'Nejla, oh God, Nejla, I can't bear it any longer.'

He began weeping almost uncontrollably. Then shaking violently, his arm began to rise until the gun was pointing at his wife.

'Hamid, *no*! Hamid, that's not the answer!' Nejla's eyes revealed the depth of her concern as she saw the despair and sense of futility in Hamid's eyes. 'Hamid, listen. Think of your child, the baby we are going to have.'

Her voice seemed to him to come from a great distance. The words seemed to pierce the inner corridors of his soul, offering hope, but then a wall seemed to loom into his vision. With tears streaming down his face, Hamid bit his lip. As if in a trance, he said, 'Nej. Oh God, why does it have to be like this?' The sound of the gun broke the silence with ruthless precision. Nejla reeled slightly backwards. Her face turned pale and her lips parted.

'Hamid?' The word was spoken quietly. An expression of pain crossed her face. Then, with great effort, she smiled tenderly, 'I love you, Hamid.'

She staggered forward and then collapsed on the floor, one hand reaching out as if to reassure her husband. A shaft of light shining through the crack in the door rested on Nejla's face, revealing the peacefulness that stayed with her as she walked through the valley of death.

Hamid's eyes stared down in disbelief and agony as the realisation of what he had done penetrated his mind. He numbly knelt down in front of her, grasped her hand and cried, 'Nejla, Nejla, my life, come back to me!'

Hearing of her sister's death, Leila had collapsed onto her knees and begun to scream. She looked upwards towards the lamp crying, 'Allah, Allah!' Then, slumping forward onto her face, she lay still, feeling she would die from the despair that totally engulfed her. She began to weep, quietly moaning, 'Nej, Nej, oh my Nejla.'

No one tried to comfort her. In the other room her mother was wailing, an eerie wail of despair and hopelessness. Her father just sat motionless, consumed by grief. Looking blankly out of the window, he held onto Nejla's teddy bear, which once had been symbolic of life, innocence, and hope.

Saturday dawned; cold, dark and raining. Hamid's mother was to be buried early in the morning. Nejla's family had expressly asked that Nejla be buried later in the day, sensing her death was the result of the cruelty of her mother-in-law.

No one turned out to mourn Hamid's mother except the *hodja* and Hussein. Only a few moments were spent at the graveside. As Hussein shovelled the earth into the grave, Hamid appeared. He was dirty and haggard. Taking a shovel, he helped his brother, but each shovelful of earth seemed only to add fuel to the fire burning in his heart. Dropping his shovel, he raced off into the rain.

That afternoon, the sun seemed to push the rain away. A great calm settled over the village. Quietly, the people made their way to the grave where Nejla was to be buried. Many were weeping openly; some in remorse for the way they had treated her, others out of genuine grief that she was gone, never to brighten their lives again with her cheerful smile.

As Leila stood by the grave, she seemed to hear words Nejla had read to her. 'I am the Resurrection and the Life. He that lives and believes in Me shall never die.' Yet now her precious sister lay lifeless in the cold earth. What kind of life was this? How could God have allowed Nejla, who was so good, to die? A burning hatred rose in her heart for Hamid. Without quite realising what she was doing she began screaming hysterically, 'I hate him, I hate him.' Then, her hands clasped to her stomach, she began to rock back and forth, moaning, 'Nejla, my Nejla. I love you so.'

Quietly Hussein went up to Leila, and gently drew her away from the crowd. Suddenly the heavens seemed to burst apart in agony and rain began to pour down. Lifting her face to the sky, the rain mingling with her tears she whispered, 'You care too, don't You, God?'

As if in answer, lightning flashed across the sky, blinding the bedraggled group, and a loud crash of thunder pealed through the heavens.

As the dawn signalled the beginning of a new day, a lonely figure could be seen kneeling at Nejla's grave. 'I'm so sorry, Nejla. You offered me life and hope and I refused them. Now it's too late for me.'

Some minutes later the same figure crawled through the rain to another fresh grave. Taking some earth in each hand and then looking at the mud as it oozed through his fingers, he said bitterly, 'That's all you ever gave me, Mother. All my hopes, my dreams, even my very life has been tainted by you and your selfish desires. Yes, I've finally realised that you are selfish. You never could bear to see anyone happy, could you? Nejla loved you. She was the only person who ever really cared about you; all the rest of us were just afraid of you. She's dead, Mother. You got your way. Are you happy?

'Well, Mother, I'm here and you're right. We won't be separated. God's garden is closed to me; instead I will share your darkness.' Hamid collapsed, weeping bitterly, then taking a deep breath and setting his face in determination he reached into his jacket. Lifting the gun to his head, he cried out, 'Forgive me, Nejla!' The sound of the gun shattered the quietness for a moment; then once again all was still in that lonely graveyard except for the patter of rain.

# 20

# *Nejla's book*

Hussein sat alone in his house smoking a cigarette in long, drawn-out drags. He too felt numb but in a different way. His sense of loss was great but his soul was weighed down with a deep burden. It was still raining for the third day in succession, and as he looked up to the sky he wondered if the town would ever know anything other than this grey, cold, damp misery.

He thought of Aysha, her husband, her brother; the tragedy of it all. He remembered the senseless killing, the bitter revenge. He thought of Serap, how harsh he had been towards her! He thought of his father; such a magnificent man in his early years, and now how his body was gradually turning to dust in the grave. His mother also haunted him; why had she been so bitter? So harsh? He thought of Hamid and Nejla. They had been happy together. What could have made his brother do such a horrible thing? Especially to hurt a girl like Nejla, who had been like a beautiful flower. Now they were both dead. Such wasted lives!

Fleetingly he thought of Leila, and moving across the room, he began to pray; 'God, I don't know if You hear me or even if I can talk to You in this way. All I know is that I need Your help. I'm so confused, there is so much that is cruel and senseless, and I need Your help to make me into a different person. Oh God, I need You but I don't know how to find You.'

Hussein walked into Hamid and Nejla's room. It didn't seem possible that just the other day they had lived together in this room. The melted stub of a candle lay to one side on the table. Nejla really tried to make things warm and friendly for Hamid, he thought to himself. He walked across to Nejla's sewing machine; she had loved to sew and work there. Lying by the side of the machine was Nejla's Bible. Hussein picked it up and flicked through its pages. Then, like a revelation that was spiritual and yet totally natural, he had an intuition that the answer to his questions was to be found in this book. This had been the source of Nejla's own understanding of God's involvement with people.

He held the book in his hand as if it were gold. His emotions began to change from an utter numbness to a growing sensation of hope. Perhaps there really were answers for him in this book! Leaving the house, and all its memories, he headed across the fields towards the clump of trees, holding onto the book, with a sense of destiny filling his mind. He made his way towards the recently cut tree stump. He had known that Hamid and Nejla had spent a lot of time by the trees, but he knew nothing of the story surrounding the cutting down of Young Love. Reaching Young Love, unaware that this stump had any significance to anyone, he sat with his back against it. Then, opening the book he was holding, he flicked through the pages and read various parts at random. Suddenly, one little passage seemed to leap out at him. 'You must be born again', it said. He stopped and looked again at the words. Jesus was speaking to a religious man; 'You must be born again'! Surely that was what he needed; to be totally reborn with a new set of values and a completely fresh start to his life! He looked up into the trees above and a sense of agony passed over him as he thought, 'Surely no one can begin life again! It's impossible.'

For several weeks Hussein spent time by the stump, reading. Then one day Hussein happened to look down towards the stump of Young Love. Sprouting up out of the side of the stump was a beautiful green shoot. The stump was producing a new tree. Then it clicked in his mind; 'Yes, that's the answer. The old tree needed to be cut down before the new shoot could grow up. I need to see God create a new life in me, as the old life is left behind,' Hussein thought as he began to search eagerly through the pages of his new-found source of wisdom, Nejla's Bible.

The room was crowded and noisy. People were talking loudly but there was very little laughter. Hussein and Leila sat behind the main table in the corner of the room. Leila's face was serious; she was trying her hardest not to spoil this important day. Her hair fell in ringlets around her face and the veil of her wedding dress rested gracefully on top of her head. She, like Nejla, was a beautiful young woman.

Leila's mother looked on, unable to join in the festivity of the moment, deep pain filling her heart. It was evident that she was still suffering greatly because of Nejla's death.

Leila's thoughts wandered back to Nejla's wedding. Then, she had been scurrying around, trying not to look at Hussein, and sharing smiles across the room with Nejla. To lose Nejla through marriage had been painful but now this total separation seemed more than she could bear. She was jarred back to the present as one of her relatives waved money three times above her head and then left it on the table. Someone had said their town was the only place to have this custom, yet vaguely she thought that she had heard of it somewhere else.

Money, what use was that? She was grateful for the gift, but could it bring Nejla back to her? Hussein sat very calmly next to her, occasionally speaking gently to her about something that was happening in the room. Yet for most of the evening, he sat silent, a look of confidence and strength on his face.

Since his encounter with God down by the tree, Hussein had given himself wholeheartedly to studying the Bible. His heart was now at peace with God. Just a few days previously he had realised, according to the Bible, how to begin life anew. In the quietness of his own room he had spoken to God and asked for forgiveness of his sins. He had wept when he thought of Jesus being crucified in his place for the punishment he deserved. Hussein had been born again.

Now Hussein looked across at Leila, who seemed

so deeply hurt by what had happened. He whispered
into her ear, 'Leila, you have done well tonight in
spite of how you feel. I'm so proud of you.' Leila
turned and looked into Hussein's face. Was this the
same man that everyone had spoken of so harshly? A
man who was bitter and cold?

'Thank you; I'm sorry I'm not being more
enthusiastic.'

'I understand,' he said with warmth. Another
relative interrupted their conversation, going through
the money-waving routine again, but now Leila felt
more relaxed.


Hussein had managed to sell the old house and
totally refurnish a new flat. As they walked through
the door, relieved to be away from the noise, Leila
was overwhelmed at the work he had put into
decorating and making it look so welcoming. She was
grateful for his thoughtfulness in protecting her from
further painful memories that would have been
caused by living in the same house where Nejla had
died so violently.

In her kitchen on the wall over the table was an
enlarged photograph of Nejla. Tears stung her eyes.
Hussein came into the kitchen holding out a parcel, 'I
have a present for you. Really, it's a present from
Nejla.'

Slowly, with stumbling fingers, and a beating
heart, Leila opened the parcel. Seeing her sister's
precious Bible, she clutched it to her heart, beginning
to sob with joy and grief. Hussein drew her into his
arms. 'I know she would have wanted you to have her

Bible. Every time you see it, it will remind you of her, and her love for you.'

The following evening, sitting together watching the glow of the fire was something new to them both. Leila felt so comfortable with Hussein that she wondered how she could ever have been frightened of him.

'Leila, something has happened to me.' His handsome face was serious as he looked tenderly at her. 'I've become a believer in Jesus.'

Leila was startled, thinking perhaps he was joking.

'What do you mean?' Leila looked wonderingly at him. Was it possible that while she had been searching in her own heart over these past few months, Hussein had also been searching? That now he was a believer like Nejla? No, surely she must have misunderstood! Answers were not to be found in belief in God. Leila shook her head as though to clear her sense of confusion. Then jumping up, stamping her foot, she exclaimed, 'A believer? In who? A God who lets cruel things happen? I will never believe in Him!' And turning, she rushed out of the room weeping.

In the morning Leila, feeling ashamed of her outburst but too shy to apologise, made a huge breakfast for Hussein. They ate quietly; then as Leila stood up to clear the table, Hussein stood as well, taking her by the hand. 'Leila, I want to show you something. Please come for a walk with me.'

The air was cool but sweet-smelling from the blossom on the trees. Winter was past and spring was well and truly here.

'Where are we going?'

'Over to a special place. A place where I began to

understand about life. See that clump of trees? Well, I met God there.'

'You met God? Surely you're joking!'

'Here, look, Leila. See this stump?' Hussein, totally taken up with how to express his thoughts, failed to see Leila's look of distress. 'Leila, this stump has become very precious to me. I come here often to think and to talk with God. You see, after Nejla's and Hamid's death I went into their room. I was so depressed and confused. Then I found Nejla's Bible. When I picked it up, I felt that it held the key that would set me free. I brought it here to this stump and spent hours reading it. Nejla had a little notebook in it with a list of verses; I read those first. One of the things that deeply troubled me was the senselessness and waste of death. I came across a verse that I have grown to love. "I am the Resurrection and the Life; he that believes in Me, though he were dead, yet shall he live." At first I was confused and even angry. Nejla believed in Him, yet now she's dead. What kind of life could that be?'

Leila listened eagerly, for he was expressing the very thoughts she had been struggling with.

'I was upset and so I got up and walked back and forth. My eyes happened to fall on this very stump that I had been leaning on. For some reason the tree had been cut down, bringing death. As I looked, I saw something amazing and wonderful. Look here, Leila. There's a new tree beginning to grow out of the old one. There must be death to be life. And see this little seed? It's only as it goes into the ground and dies, that life can come out of it. Nejla was like that tree, cut down in death. But she's not dead, she is alive with God, alive in a garden where she will never die.'

By this time, Leila was weeping brokenly. For the first time, she understood something of what Nejla had tried to teach her, realising that death was not the end but only a new beginning.

'Leila, as I looked at that stump, the thought hit me that she had to die so that I could have life. I felt completely broken, and fell to my knees and asked that Nejla's God would be my God and that He would give me His life. I have grown to love Jesus Christ because I see in Him the answer to all my desires and hopes. He *is* the Resurrection and the Life. Oh Leila, won't you let Him come in and fill the emptiness in your life? Let Him heal and cleanse you.'

For a time the only sound was Leila's sobbing. Then, looking up, she nodded her head. 'I do want to know Jesus. I have been running from Him for so long. I know you're right. I know Nejla found that He was the answer to her life.'

The young couple knelt beside Young Love. As they prayed, the birds burst out in a joyful chorus, as though thrilled by the sight of a young girl giving her life to God. As they rose from their knees, a deep sense of peace flooded Leila's heart and despite the tears on her lashes, there was a smile on her face.

Turning to Hussein, she told him with awe, 'This stump was where Nejla found God. It was a lovely tree then. Nejla often came here to read her Bible and pray. She and Hamid called it Young Love but then your mother had it cut down. Isn't it wonderful though, that love is greater than hatred or death?'

# 21

# A new joy

Looking at the glass of water on the table next to the bed made Leila's mind slip back to that dreadful morning when she had nearly swallowed the pills, hoping to end her life. Now as she lay still, yet tense, the water seemed to symbolise purity and cleansing. Nearly two years had passed since Nejla's horrible death. Hussein sat by her bed with an anxious look on his face. He hadn't slept that night and the rings under his eyes exaggerated his look of concern.

'Don't worry, darling,' Leila said, smiling reassuringly. 'It happens every day, you know.'

'Well, it doesn't happen every day to us.' Hussein looked more like a little boy waiting for a tooth to be pulled than an expectant father. Leila loved him. He was so innocent and vulnerable in some ways, yet so strong and in control in others.

'You know what these midwives can be like.'

'It's okay, Hussein, really it's okay.'

Just as she spoke a contraction began to intensify.

She breathed deeply, following the instructions in a magazine article her cousin had brought back from Germany. For a few seconds it worked, but then the intensity of the pain broke through her self-control. She strained, trying not to scream for Hussein's sake.

The thought of bringing a child into the world had thrilled them. It also left them with many anxious feelings, for this was such a confused world for a precious new life. In many ways the thought of producing something as a physical proof of their love gave them a great sense of excitement. Yet at this moment, Hussein could think of nothing else other than getting his wife through the experience. His philosophical thinking was shattered as the midwife marched into the room.

'You have to leave now, Mr Rifat.' She was a tall woman with a face that reminded him of a sergeant he once knew in his military service. Her abrupt order to leave and her grating voice made the similarity even closer.

'Everything will be fine; I love you, Hussein!' Hussein looked deep into Leila's eyes; for one panic-filled moment he wondered if this would be the last time he would see her smiling face looking back at him.

In the waiting area there was just one shabby-looking table and a chair with a broken back. An empty cigarette box lay on the table with an old newspaper. Reaching down to pick up the newspaper to help pass the time, he saw that there was one cigarette left in the box. It had been over a year now since he had smoked his last cigarette. For a moment, a surge of desire to smoke rose up in him. He took the cigarette and held it for a moment that held a universe. Then, smiling to himself, he put it back in the box. Pacing up and down was something that was expected of him in the circumstances and something that seemed a natural way to relieve his nervous energy. As he paced, he remembered his father's words when waiting in the post office for a long-distance phone call to come through.

'Any man that paces exactly six paces up and six paces down is a man who was in prison, you can always tell.'

Five, six, seven; no one was watching anyway, but somehow the association with that earlier experience seemed very real at the moment.

'Mr Rifat!' Suddenly, Hussein's reflections were shattered. He jumped as he was beckoned by the same midwife who had given him the earlier command. 'You can go in now.'

'Thank you sergeant, ah, I mean thank you.' Confusion and a fear that something dreadful had happened seemed to cloud his mind. Rushing into the hall, he ran down to the room where Leila was, hesitated for a moment before bursting through the door with determination. In the corner of the room the other midwife was clearing things away. Then his eyes focused on Leila, and he gave a huge sigh of relief. Propped up on the pillows was the face of the one he loved so dearly. Her hair was tousled and she looked pale and sleepy. She smiled with a radiance that melted his heart. Nursing gently at her breast was a beautiful little baby. As he looked at the child, he felt an immediate surge of love and identification with this little bundle of humanity.

Leila stretched out her hand. 'Come, greet our child, it's a girl.' He smiled, touched Leila's cheek, and said gently, 'I love you, Leila, I love you.' Then as Leila placed the child in his arms, he felt as if his heart would burst with joy. He enjoyed the sensation, knowing too that this was a moment he would treasure for the rest of his life.

The midwife turned and smiled. 'You are a funny couple. Happy that it's a girl? I suppose times are changing. What are you going to call her?'

Hussein turned and once again looked into his wife's deep brown eyes. Now the panic had gone. There was just awe at God's creation and this miracle of life. He turned and looked at the midwife, then smiled. 'We are going to call her Nejla.' Then, looking down into the baby's face, he touched her little cheek. 'Her name is Nejla.'

# *From the authors*

These pages have now told their story. We trust that they have helped you to see things that perhaps you have not seen before. As we look at the world today, with all its hatred and pain, perhaps we can all say that it is people like Nejla and her love that continue to give us hope to carry on. Nejla said that her strength came not from herself but from God. As we try to live in today's world, we need to see that God is real, that He does care about us as individuals, and that He wants to be involved in our lives. If you have been moved in any way by our little story, we would really love to hear from you. God has a very special plan for your life. Our prayer is that you may come to know the living God in a new and personal way.


Bob and Barbara Hitching

PO Box 17
Bromley
Kent
England